BORN TO BE MADE

Also by John Burton Thompson

Kiss or Kill
One More For The Road
Swamp Nymph

BORN TO BE MADE

JOHN BURTON THOMPSON

CUTTING EDGE

ISBN-13: 978-1-952138-31-7

Published by
Cutting Edge Publishing LLC
PO Box 8212
Calabasas, CA 91372
www.cuttingedgebooks.com

CHAPTER ONE

Marvelle Martingale was the granddaughter of a very respected minister of the gospel who, fortunately for him, had retired. Her behavior was such that no respectable congregation could have resisted hounding the kindly old man out of town.

When Marvelle was fourteen she began to wonder why boys and even grown men seemed to take scientific interest in the manner in which she walked across the campus, her head high, her carriage, even at that tender age, as graceful as any model, and her body considerably more attractive than many of the chestless, bony-faced occupants of fashion magazines. Her wonder was short-lived. One night after accepting a ride home from a movie with Cannonball Barton, the local gridiron hero, she found out in a manner that she never forgot. Cannonball thoughtfully took Marvelle's friend, Amy Gallion, home first and between Amy's house and Marvelle's there was a dark dead-end street in a new subdivision that had no houses as yet.

Marvelle discovered that his lips were honey and his hands as active as small mice and as objective as nature. She was stunned by the reaction that his caresses on her silken thighs produced, and in his expert hands, she was... not putty exactly, because putty is quiescent and Marvelle was not in the least quiescent. Cannonball had been there and she hadn't, but she seemed to know instinctively where they were headed.

He took her home that night, her body tingling and sated, her mind a vortex of emotions, so furious she almost became ill. She was not free of his goodnight embrace before she was planning an encore and with characteristic objectivity pronounced sentence on the front porch.

Her eyes were almost purple in the moonlight and her coppery blonde lashes almost obscured them as she looked at him.

"Please, C. B. Don't go yet." She was holding him tight and her body sought his, leaving no question as to what she meant.

"But ... your grandfather ... "

"He sleeps like a log. He'll never hear."

So they went into the dark living room and discovered each other all over again, nor was the darkness a deterrent. This time, however, the end result was such that her overloaded nerves couldn't stand it and she screamed shrilly, making Cannonball's concrete courage melt, leaving him white and shaking because the scream had awakened her grandfather.

She recovered swiftly, tucked her panties into her handbag and said in an undertone to him, "Let me handle this."

When her grandfather came into the living room and turned on the light, she was perched on a stout oak table with a hand at her mouth.

"Oh ... Hi, Grandpop! Sorry to wake you but you know me and mice. Just as C. B. opened the door to let me in, one ran right across the sill."

The tall, white-headed old man grunted and chuckled. "I was certain it was a Bengal tiger from the noise you made." He bent a searching look on the shaken boy. "Don't tell me you're afraid of them, too?"

Cannonball laughed nervously. "No, sir. She was the one who scared me. I thought a snake had bitten her. The ineptness of his remark caused a wave of red to flood his face and Obediah Martingale laughed.

"Well, don't let it embarrass you. Now I'm going back to bed."

The moment the door closed, she went into his arms again and he drew in a stuttering breath. "Brother, but that was a close one. Do you always do that?"

"I'm not sure. Tonight was my first time and once I did and once I didn't."

He stroked her softly firm, overpoweringly nubile body with a trembling hand and sighed. "Anyhow you sure did some quick thinking. I've heard about that I. Q. of yours. I didn't know it could be put to practical use."

She recovered quickly and was soon ready for further conquest but she discovered a fundamental weakness in the male rigging that night. Cannonball had had it and went home with his nerves still shrieking warnings.

He recovered during the night and he and Marvelle became inseparable. The joy that had been his from his other female friends was such pale provender that it ceased to interest him and the community thought the match was terribly cute. They were admired and smiled upon by their elders and everyone sighed and thought what a fine thing young love was.

Then, as elders will, they changed their minds and became almost poisonous in their antipathy to young love, stating to all who would listen that young love was spawned of the devil and headed for hell.

Cannonball Barton was considerably shaken to discover that Marvelle was his with a completeness that defied description but not to the total exclusion of all mankind. At seventeen, Marvelle was a hazard and gloried in the fact. She began to compare herself to numerous sexpot movie and TV sirens and invariably failed to suffer by comparison. She was superbly intelligent, imaginative, and curious. She was the joy of her teachers who spoke of her scholastic accomplishments among themselves, but they had begun to feel a little fearful of the heated waves of attraction that emanated from her with apparently no effort on her part at all. This was a tribute to her native ability for drama. Every move she made, every act of attraction was studied and contrived, but even at seventeen she was so convincing that no one suspected it.

It was no more than natural that an intelligent, uninhibited girl who had slain a multitude of mysteries, with a full store of confidence in her appeal to the male animal, should wish to test her arsenal. The Cannonball was no longer a test. They had made of their association a sensual parade enjoyed by both, but challenge was lacking.

Marvelle's first test was, by her own deliberate decision, the toughest that West Falls afforded. Harold Graves was the town's stalwart. He led in practically every endeavor that did not require brute strength. He was a tall, thin, bespectacled youth, very serious; so serious that girls gave him a wide berth because he was never at their mental level. He was a sober, industrious worker for his church and in all ways a model of moral decorum. This was the Gibraltar upon which Marvelle Martingale levelled her guns and the results were a visitation upon the small city that it would long remember.

The day before she had decided she would test the bastion of Harold Graves, she managed another test that was unscheduled. Spike Bordelon, an assistant coach who also taught chemistry, called her in for discussion of a paper. There was nothing whatever wrong with the paper, but Spike's French blood had been brought to a boil once too often by the sight of Marvelle walking down corridors with her free-swinging stride that activated some of her more attractive endowments in a manner calculated to do the greatest damage to male aplomb. That his career might be ruined and his neck in danger from various sources, was something Spike was past thinking about. She was a fever in his blood and a canker in his brain.

He was using the principal's office because the principal was away and he was substituting. Thus the office suggested a sort of sanctum sanctorum which, in fact, it was not, as Spike was to discover to his horror.

When Marvelle stepped into the office, she smiled mistily at the handsome stalwart Bordelon who was frowning at a paper in an effort to do something about the racing beat of his heart. She had not been unaware of his attentions for some time and had wondered idly how long it would take him to crack. She hadn't considered him as a likely subject of a test, although he was darkly attractive and was the body beautiful of the faculty. He was married and that placed him beyond her reach … a matter of which she became less and less concerned as time passed.

"Er … come in, Marvelle … come in." He was pitifully agitated, so she agitated him more by walking with slow deliberate steps to a chair and sitting. Her hip sway was exaggerated the tiniest bit, just enough to make it look deliciously natural. Her waist was tiny, her hips swiveled on a spine that was as flexible as a switch. She sat with fluid grace that Spike winced with something like a real pain. She wore a russet skirt and a matching sweater that could do nothing to obscure the valorous leap of her breasts and just before entering the office she had opened another button and the result was everything she might have hoped.

"I called you about this paper," he began, hating the catch in his throat and the tricks his respiration was playing on his speech.

"Oh…" Her thick, swallow-winged eyebrows went up in a smooth motion that was sheer dramatic witchery. "Did I do something wrong?"

"No, as a matter of fact, you didn't. The paper is perfect…"

"Then, what is the…"

"Nothing the matter at all. Just a really fine paper, and I wanted to congratulate you on it."

This was such a palpably spurious excuse that she became a little excited since she was certain that the paper had had nothing to do with the summons and that left but one other thing. With the test of Harold Graves in the near offing, she thrilled to the prospect of flexing some of her vast store of armament. She caught the straight chair by the seat on either side of her smoothly curved thighs and hitched herself forward a fraction in order to allow a kind of semi-stretch which shoved her high, hard breasts almost out of the plunging neckline. Slowly she relaxed, watching the expressions chase themselves across his face.

"That was really very nice of you," she murmured with a soft throatiness that made his mind veer crazily. She relaxed but he retained the picture of a lacy edged bra so filled with creamy smooth flesh as to almost overflow.

He shrugged. "If you'd handed in a bad paper. I would have called you in, so I thought if I'm to be fair, I must congratulate good students as well as criticize the bad."

"I think that's very nice, Mr. Bordelon. It looks like..." She got up and approaching, rested her hands on the desk. She smiled apologetically. "It seems as though good students are taken for granted, but just make a mistake and you get a roasting."

"A flaw in our system," he snapped shakily.

"At least you're not following it." she said so softly that his eyes stung. "May I go now?'

"Yes, er ... that is ... do you want to go?" He heard himself saying it from afar as though it was someone else, but why shouldn't she? After all, could he chance anything in the principal's office? Of course, not. Maybe he'd just use this as an entering wedge. The thought was a relief but in the act of getting up to see her out of the door she answered his question."

"No ... I'm not in a hurry to go."

The words were not exceptional but the melting quality in her violet eyes, the breathless look on her face, the moist hunger that trembled on her full, smooth lips shocked him to the quick ... and then she was in his arms and he never knew if it was her's or his own efforts that effected the embrace. She was tall and slender and so excitingly hard-soft that his mind reeled and her lips seemed on the verge of stealing his soul from his body.

He pressed her close and the shock was intensified by the fact that she flowed like soft mastic into every line of his body and the invitation was unmistakable. It was then that Spike

Bordelon lost command of the situation. He forgot where he was ... where they were. He forgot everything but this burning morsel in his arms and the lips that were driving him to within range where the warm contact of her body took over and sent him completely over the precipice. He moved her without being aware of it to the office couch. His left hand slid upward along one glistening thigh and Miss Emily Carstairs opened the door on the most fundamental guttural she had ever heard come from a girl's throat.

Miss Emily was an English teacher about fifty years old and comfortably secure in middle-aged spinsterhood. She stopped short, gasped from a shock that made her tingle from head to toe in a manner that she had left behind some thirty years ago, and it was her frantic effort to shut the door ... which sounded like a major explosion that brought them back to reality.

She stood bereft of speech for a moment and managed to note that Marvelle merely slid away, her skirt slipping down into place, then she stood and regarded the teacher through fathomless violet eyes.

Spike Bordelon, however, looked like he had been subjected to sudden high voltage. He went a sickly pale and raised a palsied hand that hung cataleptically until Miss Emily managed to speak.

"This," she said in her clipped precise way, "would have been rather touching had it not involved considerable more intimacy than a mere ... a mere ..." Her vocabulary deserted her momentarily. "And a married man," she finished with a rush.

The assistant coach groaned, sinking into a chair where he felt he would become actively ill. His career was blasted and black doom stared him in the face. He could see screaming headlines about a teacher in disgrace, attempting to ravish who was probably the town's loveliest maiden. Suicide was a mortal sin and he would be refused the rites of the Church. It would settle everything, but it was unthinkable.

Miss Emily looked at him for a moment and to Marvelle it seemed that her eyes were sad rather than critical. This must be a mistake, but it was there to see.

She turned to the girl and said in a low voice, "Come with me, my dear."

Marvelle followed her out and into the first aid room where Miss Emily shut and locked the door. When she faced the girl she felt a flit of annoyed panic. There was not the slightest sign of repentance on Marvelle's face. Instead, now, it had hardened into a mask of nothingness, the usually melting eyes slaty and opaque.

"Sit down, child."

Marvelle obeyed, her face still expressionless. "I think I can recite what you're going to say, Miss Emily. Maybe I can save you the trouble. If you blame him all the way. you're wrong."

"Why did you get me in here?"

It was not an easy question to answer. The lurid tableau still had a part of Miss Emilys usually agile mind stumbling around in circles trying to find some kind of order. "Maybe," she said with badly repressed agitation, "I'd better tell you what I am not going to say. Maybe that'll be easier, will make you understand me better and give me something to say while I'm getting over that scene. First, I'm not going to say anything outside of this room. You needn't tell Muscle Boy about it for a while. I want him to stew a little. Maybe if he knows he's stupid and to what extent, he may be able to avoid the more poisonous aspects of it in the future."

Marvelle stirred and her face lost some of its immobility. "You mean you're going to let it drop ... just like that?"

Miss Emily nodded. "I think I can understand your disbelief. It isn't what you'd expect out of a small-town, old maid teacher, but I must tell you that I was not always an old maid in mind and, though it might stretch your belief, I was quite a chick in my day."

"I'd have no trouble in believing that you were beautiful, Miss Emily. In fact, I think you're quite nice to look at now."

Thank goodness she didn't lay it on too thick, thought Miss Emily, or I'd have thrown her out...and she believes what she's saying.

"Thank you," said Miss Emily turning pink. "I merely told you that because I haven't trod the severely narrow myself, and I know something about ecstasies even if I was too ignorant to take what was mine and some other, more enterprising chic, stole my man from me." Miss Emily straightened and improved the line of her front considerably. She was comfortably fleshed and only her face told the story of years of frustration, the bridling of passions and subsequent suffering. "Marvelle, I'm going to ask you a personal question, so personal you might not wish to answer. It that is the case, you are free to keep silent..."

"No, Miss Emily, I'm not a virgin and haven't been since I was fourteen."

The teacher gaped for a second, somewhat put out of countenance. "How did you know...?"

"It was natural. I suppose a good many people are wondering."

Miss Emily sighed and slumped again. "Well, I wondered. In there you didn't seem at all out of your depth. Not nearly as much as he did. I just wondered. Thank you for telling me."

"You're not going to read me a sermon?"

"Would it do any good?"

The girl thought for a moment, then lifted her eyes. "If you've been there yourself and taking my personality into consideration, do you think it would?"

"No, I don't think it would, and I'm not going to tell you anything." She got up and stood over the girl, her eyes damp, her heart aching with a strange, poignant affection. " I just hope, Marvelle, that you'll never regret any of this. I hope it doesn't ruin you and make you hard and unfeeling."

Marvelle stood up with quick impulsiveness and kissed the pale lips. "Miss Emily, neither you nor I can predict the future. I'll just have to wait and see ... and I love you because you're being wonderful about this and because you even care. A lot of people wouldn't ... and don't."

Miss Emily blinked away the tears. "I ought to smack your bottom, said the teacher tremulously. "I'm a fool for letting you get under my skin but, dammit, I love you, too, and have ever since you've been taking English under me. Child, you're too sensitive to ever get hard and uncaring. I can see that sensitivity come out in every theme you write. You dig so deep into the fundamentals that I can hardly believe that you're just a senior, even if you are nearly eighteen. I've told you this before, you're a born writer. Tell me, do you like it?"

"I love it. I hate grammar and syntax but I just love themes. I seem to get a release ... and I even write when there's no assignment. Sometimes I have the theme already written, then you come up with a subject where it'll fit and I shove it in."

"Yes," grumbled Miss Emily, "I thought some of them looked a trifle yellowed and smelled musy. Well, go about your business and just for me, be careful.

"All I can say is thank you, Miss Emily. Just think what would have happened if it had been a couple of others we can think of."

"Yes. I know very well what a stew would have been raised. A perfectly good if stupid man would have lost his job and his reputation. When I look at you I wonder how many will fall into his same blunder."

"Do you know Harold Graves?"

"I should. He's in one of my classes, the smart, smug, self-centered, sanctimonious ninny. Why?"

Marvelle smiled mysteriously. "I wonder if he's as good as he thinks he is?"

"I doubt it and if anyone could find out, I'd say it would be you. Don't tell me ..."

"I think I'll find out if he's really good or just thinks he is."

Miss Emily chuckled and sighed. "My God, Emily Carstairs can stand here and listen to you plot a man's downfall and never turn a hair ... even feel a little excited about it. Go on and get out of here ... and let me know how you manage."

Marvelle kissed her again. "I'm glad I didn't leave school before I found out what a wonderful person you are, Miss Emily." She left then and Emily Carstairs stood silently for a long time, regretting a number of things that she hadn't allowed to happen to herself.

She was not an essentially a cruel woman and after Marvelle left, she went back to the principal's office and walked in. Spike was seated at the desk, a look of death in his eyes.

"Well," she began acidly, "what have you to say for yourself?"

He lifted suffering eyes. "Say?" he croaked. "What is there to say?"

"Oh ... maybe that she's been on your trail for weeks and finally caught you at a weak moment, that once she started in on you, you didn't have a chance ... that it's all her fault. Things like that."

He clenched his big hands slowly. "Miss Carstairs, if I uttered a single word along those lines, it wouldn't be true."

She cocked her head on one side and nodded pertly. "Well, at least you're honest and for that reason, along with a few others that don't concern you, I hereby make you the solemn promise that not a single word of this will pass my lips. I suppose every man has his limits."

A sudden weakness seemed to flow through Spike's frame and before it reduced him to shuddering hysteria, Miss Emily turned and left the office. Spike caught his face in his hands and wept with a quiet deadly intensity for some time.

CHAPTER TWO

It goes without saying that Harold Graves didn't have a chance, but not even Marvelle could have foreseen the end results because she hadn't known how completely Harold's mind had been kept in seclusion to the extinguishment of everything except good works and scholastic matters. It is possible that she caught him at the moment of belated awakening or that she hastened the inevitable a little but one thing is certain he was never the same again.

It happened with a casualness that few could have arranged but Marvelle and this she did with her usual exacting care.

He was such a creature of habit that she knew the table in the library where he invariably studied his chemistry. It was near the chemistry references and he knew their titles by heart. No one ever sat at the table because he always affected a superior attitude which the girls hated. He made the boys feel like intellectual clods and girls preferred richer fields.

He didn't fully realize she was there for some time, being vaguely conscious that some other human was across the table, but the impression bore no identification. What it was that reached out between them and caused him to look up is not known, but he did raise his eyes and the sight that presented itself almost startled an exclamation from him. She was absorbed in a book spread before her, her slim smooth-skinned hands crossed at the wrists and upon her forearms her exciting breasts rested. She wore another sweater but one no more able to conceal than the one which caused Mr. Bordelon to lose his head, and again one more button was undone than should have been. Harold's mouth fell open and stayed for some time. His eyes bored into the creamy hemispheres with such concentration that she had raised her eyes and had watched him for some time before he was aware that she had noticed, then he nearly fainted from mortification.

"Are you ill, Harold?" she asked in a undertone.

Harold made several noises, none of which could have been called a reply, and she used his incoherence as an excuse to get up and come around to his side of the table, a situation from which he might have fled had not one end of the table been against the wall effectively blocking any flight.

"I didn't understand you," she said in an undertone that sent his already hammering pulse into conniptions.

"I," he managed to get out finally, "didn't say anything. I was staring at you ... I don't know why, but I was. You caught me and it embarrassed me. I'm sorry. I beg your pardon."

"For looking at me?"

"Well ... in the most exact sense, that's what I mean and yet it is not ... precisely."

"That sounds a little abstruse."

He was surprised to hear her use such a word. To him women were all dull and stupid. "I suppose it does ..."

"Then you mean you were staring at some particular part of me." She arched her back and the leaping revolution of her breasts which the act brought into sharp staggering definition almost took his breath. Unaccountably he became emboldened.

"Well, must admit that what you say is true."

"Then what's so bad about that? Your attention was very flattering. I'm not sure that I'm not the only girl at school you've ever paid attention.'

"The only one. Absolutely the only one. Not another single solitary one ..." He stopped because he sounded silly even to himself, and he was conscious of a strange, sweet desire to be anything but silly before this gorgeous creature with the shiny red-gold hair and the melting violet eyes.

"Then see? That flatters me. I like to be flattered." She glanced around swiftly then back at him. "Thank you, Harold ... so *much.*" She bent and kissed him fleetingly on the lips and left him.

Such was his reaction that his study period was nearly over before he realized that he hadn't done any work at all. This was appalling and the rest of that day he spent trying to catch glimpses of her and wondering what it was that had turned his mind so diametrically away from his studies.

He went home in a rosy haze, oblivious to everything but the way Marvelle's skirt fitted her trim but sufficient hips, the seductive sway of them as she walked, making the skirt sort of switch in a very restrained manner, the way her breasts had looked half revealed by the sweater, pushed up even higher by her forearms. And she liked him. He had flattered her. She admitted as much, so why shouldn't she like him? After these thoughts took hold, Harold began to strut. His mother had tried to get him interested in girls, but he resisted her for a number of reasons, large among which loomed the lack of courage. He never admitted to this, however.

He noticed her for the first time Wednesday morning. He suffered, unable to study or think of anything else until Saturday night when he decided he'd have to tell someone about her or his emotions would deal him mortal injury, so he told his mother.

She was overjoyed and insisted that he bring the girl ... she vaguely remembered that the Rev. Martingale had a grand-daughter who lived with him, to dinner. This was expeditiously arranged for Sunday night and Cannonball Barton had to go looking elsewhere for entertainment, a matter that occasioned him considerable annoyance, not to say dismay. It was not the first time he had sensed that his magnetism was losing some of its power.

Mrs. Graves, plump, pink and inclined to be fluttery, so vexed her son at dinner that he felt a desire to scream because she monopolized the conversation, asking Marvelle innumerable questions, some of them of a rather personal nature which embarrassed him. Such as just what her social life amounted to, with whom, and the like. Marvelle either answered her directly or deftly parried questions she didn't care to answer, and was in all ways so considerate and sweet to the older woman that Harold, in spite of his annoyance, adored her for it. He scarcely ate anything at all and was so nervous when the dessert came, that he almost wept with relief.

Since Bertha Graves had long been convinced that her son could do no wrong, since his breeding did not allow for it, she had no qualms whatever about making an unscheduled visit to her sister who lived across town. She was so overjoyed with Harold's choice of a girl that she felt it only fair that they have privacy.

Harold shared this opinion up to the time he saw the door close, then he was almost carried away by panic. He had no knowledge of what a boy and girl did when alone, but he was unnecessarily worried. Marvelle had no intention of allowing the situation to become sticky.

"What a lovely phonograph," she said and got up, walked over to it and examined it with the eye of a connoisseur. He followed her.

"Yes, it's quite expensive, but I'm afraid we don't have any good popular music."

"Oh … the classics, some tangos and rhumbas that my sister bought before she went to college."

"Try the rhumbas. Maybe we can dance to them."

"I'm afraid I'm not well versed in the intricacies of the dance."

She turned and smiled so heatedly at him that he blushed. "Neither am I, rhumba-wise, but since we'll both be learning, maybe it'll be fun." For some time Marvelle had practiced the rhumba in her room while alone and more often than not, nude. She had some rather original ideas as to how it should be done and though her ideas would have received whole-hearted support in Cuba. American society is not yet ready for the heated convolutions necessary to this sort of music. The rhumba, when done as it should be, is a page straight from the Kinsey Report.

Harold Graves found this out and allowed himself to be led into a rather orgiastic dance which seemed particularly suited to the slippery footwork of Marvelle as well as to the flexible witchery of her body.

Marvelle thought wisely that this was it, and pounced surely. She went into his arms and now he was certain that she knew. Since it was impossible that she not know, he became emboldened and kissed her, encircling her in a torrid embrace but he was not prepared for the kiss that followed. It all but unhinged his reason and another betrayal even worse than the first, reduced him to trembling apathy so she led him to the couch where the night for Harold simply went to pieces. Things happened so naturally and so easily that afterward he couldn't recall with any clarity the details, but it was an ecstatic nightmare of sensation, of honeyed lips and darting tongue, of wild heated embraces, of shrill cacophonic music. Just how it was that it all began with them fully dressed and ended without either of them having on anything, was another thing he could never remember. Marvelle had thoughtfully doused the only light out of respect for his modesty ... not hers, and she eventually proved conclusively that Harold Graves was not the kind of man both he and the rest of the town had assumed.

Bertha Graves' sister was not home and after a couple more abortive attempts at visiting, she sighed, went to Handley's Drug Store, had a soda, then took herself home.

When she turned on the light, it was several seconds before her slightly myopic vision could focus and several more seconds before her stunned sense could credit what she saw on the couch. Some measure of their enchantment might be assessed by the fact that neither of them was actually and consciously aware that the light had been turned on and that they had a visitor.

Harold, when he did realize that his mother was staring at them, that they were in a position often euphemistically described as comprising, that his mother's mouth was slack with horror and her hair was figuratively standing on end, did something that had been lurking very close for several days. He screamed, leaped to his feet and fled in blind panic.

Bertha's Victorian brain had absorbed all it could in one night and she slipped to the floor in a swoon. Marvelle, her breasts heaving slightly but . unperturbed, dressed with deliberation and casually walked out of the front door. She took a deep breath of cool night air and started walking home.

Had Bertha Graves been possessed of a fraction of the open-minded tolerance of Miss Emily Cartairs, a great deal of the resultant furor might have been avoided, or at least confined to the proper channels. Since she did not and since she believed Harold's story of rape, she went luridly berserk and the shock to the town was something to see. Marvelle, naturally, became a pariah and respectable people turned from her as though she had a dread disease.

Miss Emily Carstairs, hearing of the plot to refuse the girl her high school diploma, promptly went on the warpath. Her first ally she was certain of and in the hall one morning stopped Spike Bordelon.

"Spike, since we both know who and what I'm talking about, I won't waste words. I know there isn't much you can do positively, but I shall expect every word in defense of Marvelle getting her diploma at your limited command. Do I make myself perfectly clear?"

Spike blushed to the roots of his dark hair. "Yes *ma'am*, Miss Carstairs. As you say, there isn't much I can do, but I'll do my best. You can depend on it."

"I shall," she retorted grimly.

The principal was a harassed man who didn't know what to do and said as much. "After all, I've got the public and the school board to consider."

"I consider the public fools and the school board fools with the added stature of asses. Since I'm sure you won't agree, and since such a statement will have no weight, you have my permission to forget it. Just the same, the spectacle Bertha Graves has made of the matter and the subsequent reaction of the population of West Falls, lends support to my contention."

"That may all be true, Emily, but what can we do?"

"Has there been any official action by the school board?"

"No…not yet. I've spoken to several of them. They seem to be in agreement that she shouldn't be allowed to continue in school."

"I doubt that she'd care a lot about that. She can pass any test any member of your faculty can devise on any subject. Her grades for the past five years will support that statement. It will be the cruelest persecution if that child is denied her diploma. I'm going to see her grandfather."

"What good will that do?"

"None probably, but I want him and her to know that not everyone in West Falls is without a little human kindness." She looked at him for a moment. "You know something, Abel, I could give you a stroke right now if I had something against you."

"Me…how?"

"Well, once…sometime in the past several years, you had a man teacher right here in school that came within an inch of doing just what Harold Graves did. I walked in on them."

Abel Hacket flushed violently "My God," he breathed desperately. "Who else knows?"

"No one. Neither do you. I'll go to my grave with the secret and you'll go to yours wondering."

"Then," he said virtuously, "maybe she's just as Mrs. Graves described her."

"You tottering sanctimonious ass," she shouted, losing her temper. "Since when did men…one grown with children of his own the other ready to graduate from high school…since when have they been so damned hard to rape?" Her voice rose to almost a scream and Mr. Hackett strove hard to shush her, fearing that someone would hear. She subsided eventually but flounced out of the office still fuming with rage.

Although several of the school board members had ideas of their own that did not coincide with popular opinion, none of them had the courage to come to Marvelle's defense actively. So in order to have things done with a great pretense of fairness and little damage to the school board members, a special meeting was called to sort of hash things out to the greatest advantage of all. Two men, not members, were called in presumably to advise, actually in the faint hope that the school board might in some manner hand these two prominent men a very hot potato.

One was Ezekiel Highsmith, the local judge, a very learned and some said, hard man. Some said he looked like Abe Lincoln. All agreed that he was very tall, bony and ugly. The other was a retired doctor, Hadron Myles, a psychiatrist by virtue of a long life of practice among the mentally ill in the State Mental Institution and the "Grandfather Clause" in board requirements.

"This should be something," said Dr. Myles to the judge as they took their seats together in the meeting room.

"What's it all about?" asked the cadaverous Highsmith stroking his long jaw.

"Hell, ain't you heard? Marvelle Martingale raped Harold Graves." The doctor chuckled sarcastically. "They don't seem to think they can make the charge stick, or I'm sure they'd have arrested her. Next best thing to do is stop her diploma." The doctor settled his enormous bulk in his chair and scrabbled irritably in his tumbling grey hair. He pouted and lit a cigar.

"Um ..." murmured the judge, his deep-set eyes lighting with interest. "So that's it. They want us to place the seal of approval on the act?"

"Something like that. I'm too old to give a damn what this bunch of jerks think and as far as I'm concerned, Bertha just came home too soon. That Marvelle is a gal I'd like to have known at the age of eighteen. I've seen so much of the seamy side of life to get my dander up because a couple of kids get caught doing what comes naturally. *Caught*, I said ... get me?"

"Who better than me?" rumbled the judge. "I've been on the bench thirty years and practiced before then."

Bertha Grave was not present but the president of the school board read a long rambling letter from her to the board explaining in confused and repetitious detail what had occurred. The president then folded the letter and turned to the board.

"So, gentlemen, we are here to decide what punishment should be meted out to this wayward girl. With us, we are fortunate to have, the learned District Judge, Ezekiel Highsmith and a retired psychiatrist, Dr. Hadron Myles. They have agreed to answer any questions we might want to ask."

Judge Highsmith stood to the limit of his imposing height. "I should like to remind this august group of one thing. There may be no questions that will come to your minds. In that event I shall feel free to speak if I desire."

"By all means, Judge ... by all means. You may have the floor any time you desire it."

"In that case I feel I should say right now that you have just made an unfortunate statement. Am I correct in assuming that the minutes of this meeting are being transcribed?"

"You are, sir. That is Miss Judkin's job." He waved toward a wispy blonde who was making shorthand notes. "What do you mean, Judge ... an unfortunate remark?"

"Just this, sir. You have read a letter purportedly written by one Bertha Graves. May I ask if it is a deposition?"

"If you mean was it taken before a notary, as a statement, no sir. It is a personal letter written in long hand to this body."

"Then it is not evidence and any action taken upon it is legally invalid insofar as said action is dependent upon the letter. Moreover, any action taken upon the strength of this letter will be actionable by the … um … I almost said defendant … the girl. As I have said, it is not evidence. I must also remind this body that although it has gathered to punish one Marvelle Martingale, it is not the opinion here that you are a group constituted to punish. I am under the distinct impression that punishment of any criminal act rests squarely with the courts as set forth by the constitution of this sovereign state. In the event that you do follow a line of punishment, then I must advise again that your actions may and probably will be liable and if the girl seeks legal redress all sorts of unpleasant contingencies could be forthcoming."

The judge sat down amid a fearful silence and crossed his bony hands. The only sounds were the uncontrolled chuckles of Dr. Myles. "You sound like a hod-gasted politician but it sure was beautiful. Oh brother, was it beautiful, even if it did sound like a politician."

"It so happens," murmured the judge under his breath, "that I am a politician. You think I'm spreading all this sonorous wind just to hear the noise I make?"

"Look at the president. I think he got hold of a bad oyster."

Mr. Jackson, the president, was suffering from within. He changed color several times and conceived an acute distaste for the men who sat before him as still as crawfish mounds waiting for him to reply to the judge's devastating remarks. Mr. Jackson, belatedly realized that he had gotten off on the wrong foot, that the whole thing was a mess and that it was a political mistake to bend too readily to public opinion which was as changeable as the cone of a tornado.

"Well," squeaked Mr. Jackson, wiping his bald spot with a trembling hand, "I'm not sure I said anything about a criminal charge."

The judge again stood slowly, ponderously, dramatically. "I think you mentioned punishment. If the girl has done nothing criminal, what is it you wish to punish her for? Before you answer, I think I must remind you, one and all, that I will have no part in what now appears to be persecution traveling under the thin guise of prosecution, which, I again remind you, is not inherent to your powers as a school board."

Mervin Jenkins, a member who was an agitator and had fanned the flame more than other said, "Are you going on record as approving of the girl's actions?"

"No sir, I do not approve. Neither do I disapprove. I have no opinion on the matter whatever. So far there has not been shown one shred of proof that anything happened."

"You're forgetting the letter," bleated Mr. Jackson triumphantly.

"I'm not forgetting the letter, Mr. Jackson, and I hope you never come into my court bearing as evidence anything so absolutely shorn of any resemblance to it as the letter. You have read a bitter tirade written by a mother. I don't know what she saw and it is not easy to arrive at, by what she has written. You all seem to feel that an accusation is all that is needed for conviction. It might be well if you borrowed a few volumes of Blackstone and boned up. You've heard the mother. Have you heard the girl?"

Mr. Jackson fidgeted and felt like a fool. "Well... no, we haven't."

"And May I ask why?"

Mr. Jackson was in pain. "We are not lawyers, Judge. We were trying to do what had been suggested to us within the scope of our powers."

"It is patently apparent that you're not lawyers, although if you persist along these lines, I fear you will have need of several of them. Character assassination, using unsupported hearsay parading as evidence, is a dangerous undertaking. If you don't believe me, ask any lawyer. I also fear that you have misinterpreted your own powers."

Mr. Jackson paled and pulled at his lower lip. "Then you advise that we do nothing further about this? That we do not try to withhold her diploma?"

"Such approximately is my advice. As a matter of fact, should the girl take this proposed action to a court of law ... and it could be done, I fear that you would have to prove that she raped Harold Graves. Even in that unlikely event, I fear that you could still not withhold her diploma. I am somewhat surprised that a group of grown men could entertain such an idea since the very thought of the charge implies physical attack and subsequent defeat of the man involved. Assuming, in an outside eventuality, that such could occur, then there is another thing which I think you have not taken into consideration. There are certain male physical requirements to rape which should they prove possible under physical attack and defeat, would constitute a very rare phenomenon indeed. You gentlemen, in addition to subjecting yourselves to legal action, would certainly become the laughing stock of the county. I advise you think it over."

He sat down again amid more silence and this time Dr. Myles' laughter was plainly audible.

"Zeke, what a pity this masterly oration doesn't get wider circulation."

Judge Highsmith tilted his head over to a side seat where a newspaper reporter was scribbling furiously over his copy pad. "What make you think it won't?"

Dr. Myles looked and almost exploded. "Oh my ... Oh my ... Oh my. Zeke, let's go sample some of that twenty-year-old bourbon you keep hidden in your chambers."

"I think that'd be a good idea," said the judge, and they got up and walked slowly out.

CHAPTER THREE

Harold Graves was actively ill and confined to his bed. Bertha Graves wondered if she could ever hold up her head again. The story had hit the newspapers and although the town still boiled, it boiled in two factions now, instead of one. The dividing line was nebulous and opinions still swapped sides as gossip grew, but Marvelle Martingale received her diploma with the rest of the class, her head high, her big violet eyes flashing, her stride graceful and sure, her middle swaying just a shade more than it should.

Miss Emily Carstairs giggled and sobbed at the same time, her eyes obscured by tears. Mr. Hackett, the principal, collapsed in his seat and wiped a deposit of sweat from his neck. Mr. Jackson, who had to make the graduation address, forgot his lines three times and dropped his reference cards twice. When he finally got through it, he went home and got steaming drunk.

While West Falls simmered and snapped, a series of circumstances began to unwind which was to change the life of Marvelle Martingale.

A New Yorker, name of Edward Briarcliffe Colton the Third, occupation, gentleman opportunist, happened to be driving along the federal highway that serves West Falls when something in the inner workings of his sleek Alfa-Romeo went haywire. It was a small thing and its very smallness was one reason why Hagler's Garage didn't stock the part. So Edward Colton was faced with a two-day wait while the part, an insignificant portion of the ignition system, about the size of a small brooch, was being flown in from New York. His soul curdled with

He asked and was directed to The Top Hat, an emporium dedicated to the slaking of thirst. He found it dim, cool and quiet. He was about to enjoy further hospitality of West Falls when a vision floated before his eyes when he was going into the place.

He ordered a tall glass of Teacher's and water at the bar and brooded over the vision for a while.

"Beg pardon," began Colton hesitantly.

"Friend, I'm a stranger in town."

"Sure," said Gus, displaying a set of teeth that could have crushed the thigh bone of a steer.

"Sure," agreed Gus, giving him a careful appraisal. He approached six feet in height, his features regular and pleasing, his skin clear and well groomed. His straight black hair lay back on his symmetrical head without protest. His clothes were conservative, well-cut and spoke of an expensive tailor.

"Sure," said Gus again. "What can I do for you."

"You can keep me out of trouble."

Gus chuckled. "Well, wont nobody bother you 'less you get rambunctious."

"I just want to ask a simple question that I know you can answer. I mean no disrespect to the party involved, but just as I was walking in, I saw a girl and a young man pass in a car. Just what kept me from stumbling and falling I don't know. Now I live in New York. Beautiful women come and go like flies. This one was something more than that. She, sir, crossed my eyes and I almost ran into your entrance door. There couldn't be two like her in West Falls. If there are, I'm going to become a permanent resident. As I say, I mean no disrespect and I'm not being nosey just for the hell of it."

Gus laughed aloud. There were no other patrons this early and he was glad of a chance to talk about Marvelle Martingale without offending a faction.

"Well, 't wont take no thought on the matter. We got our share of good lookers but Marvelle makes them look like scrub-women. That was Marvele Martingale and Cannonball Barton. She stirred up some little stink not long ago. Got the town bitin' at itself all over."

"That I can believe," agreed Colton profoundly. "Mind telling me about it?"

"Well... no. 'Taint a secret, so to speak." Gus Evans was imaginative, tolerant and an unsung raconteur. When he was finished, Colton couldn't remember ever having been so intrigued.

"Now that is something for the books," he breathed, lighting a cigarette. He extended his hand. "Ed Colton... Mr ...?"

"Evans... Gus Evans." Colton's hand was engulfed and nearly pulverized by Gus' gigantic paw. "Pleased t' meetcha."

Colton flipped his hand gingerly several times under the cover of the bar and worked his fingers experimentally. "Likewise," he replied and almost blushed. "What do you think happened?"

"Well, I've known 'em both since they was kids. One sure thing, Marvelle didn't invite herself to the Graves' house. She didn't walk in uninvited. The boy is one of these book worms and I sorta got an idea that he woke up one day and there she was. I can 'magine what that'd do to a boy who never thought about women before... sorta startin' at the top, if you know what I mean. So he managed to invite her to the house. She accepted and... well, I don't know what happened to Bertha, but all of a sudden they found themselves alone. They was alone when the water begun to rise and before he knew what was what, he was in over his head. Bertha said she caught 'em on the sofa. Maybe she did, but the attitude has been all over that the girl was at fault until Judge Highsmith threw the lash at the school board and made them back water. Now she's been goin' out with Cannonball Barton, the all-state fullback for two, three years and I know him. I'd make book that she knew a lot more than Harold Graves when the chips was down."

"What'll she do since she's graduated?"

"Beats the hell out of men. She's good looking' enough to mighty near write her own ticket. Looks like you got one all blank and ready for the pen yourself."

"Mr. Evans, you're a man of great penetration. I salute your perspicacity."

Gus nodded happily. "Thanks. It all comes from bartendin'. Wasn't for the medical society, all retired bartenders would hang up psychiatrists' shingles."

It is not recorded just what methods Edward Briarcliffe Colton the Third used to entice Marvelle Martingale into his toils, but it was accomplished. Marvelle was a natural victim, her vision being on vague and distant horizons, her natural leaning toward things sensual and fleshy. It must be assumed that Edward plied her with a variety of blarney to which she was unaccustomed so that when he proposed a halt in their journey for food and drink, she was past the need for either as far as his purpose was concerned.

"Beg pardon," he asked politely. He hadn't forgotten to be polite, knowing that small town people place a great store by the gesture.

She was dressed in dark blue woolen slacks and a turtle neck sweater. She twisted in the seat to face him. "I was thinking of that line you handed Grandpop ... he didn't even manage any good objections."

Edward grinned personably. "I painted a picture of you and the modeling world, the advantages of the big city, the stifling effect of the small town on your personality ... your recent brush with propriety ..."

She sobered. "He was really swell about that. It seems that Grandpop spent most of his life ranting and bellowing from the pulpit about the weaknesses of humanity. Then he discovered that what he had been calling weaknesses were the human animal at work and I think he sort of wishes he'd gone about it differently."

"No doubt," commented Edward, not caring to delve too deeply into philosophy at the moment. "This looks like a good place." He swung the sleek car off the road and stopped it beneath a modernistic concrete canopy that afforded patrons protection from inclement weather.

Their meal was delightful, as were the martinis before and the Scotch and water afterward, and by the time he registered them as man and wife at a very plush motel a few miles further on, Marvelle was not in the mood for the double nature of the sleeping arrangements which Edward had decided upon because of a quirk of his nature. He had gotten a double cabin and showed every intention of utilizing it as such. It would tickle his vanity to make her come to him.

This was their first moment alone under conditions that were right for her to exercise intentions which she had thought about long before bed arrangements had been mentioned. She came from the bath wrapped to the chin in a white wooly robe that suggested her nubility with such throat-aching subtlety that Edward felt a little faint. He was forced to drop his casual man-of-the-world attitude and never quite recovered it again. She stopped and watched him come up from his position on the other bed. His eyes were a little glassy as he approached her and if he expected her to play coy he was disappointed. She came naturally and easily into his arms and his embrace lacked some of the finesse he usually managed to maintain consciously.

Marvelle was very elementally constituted and when her lips touched his, he, too, became a rag in the teeth of a desire that did not allow for much in the way of tactics. He dropped to her level with such ease that the sound in his throat that spoke of something approaching delirium almost startled him. He tore away by main force and plunged into the bathroom. She sat on her bed, her eyes dreamy and a little half smile twitching one corner of her mouth.

When he returned, also dressed in a robe, he forgot about making her come to him and reversed the procedure nor was he surprised when he discovered that she wore nothing under her robe. It was a night he would not soon forget. She was a serpent that writhed and twisted and managed him with steely unbelievable strength. She was a trollop and a virgin, she was tender and bruising, her lips soft and sweet but her teeth were ravening and twice brought blood of which he was only dimly aware. She was soft and hard, she was a shaft of Elgin marble and a python. She was a courtesan and a pagan priestess and when at long last nature sought rest from its stupendous demands, Edward lay on his side still holding her close, tears running from his eyes for the first time since he had become a man.

He was in a hurry to get to New York but the trip which normally would take two or three days was stretched to five and even then he gritted his teeth at the sight of the Holland Tunnel entrance.

Then his mind began to function, something it had done only in fits and starts since that first night. His aunt had a nice apartment on East Fifty-seventh and she was in Florida for the winter. He had the key and free use of it. His allowance, while generous, was not sufficient for an apartment of the sort he wanted for his mistress and still allow for his standard of living. He sighed happily and the tunnel did not scowl at him now.

"There's one thing we haven't mentioned," said Marvelle, thinking of the same thing at the same time.

"what's that?"

"Where'll I stay and what'll I do?"

He chuckled. "You stay in a really nice apartment and you'll do nothing but love me." He hugged her close for a moment.

"The apartment sounds fine," she agreed, "but I want to work."

"Why? There'll be no need for it. You'll just lounge around and stay pretty for me."

She looked at him dispassionately, something he found unaccountably annoying. Her eyes were cool and calculating. 'I'm afraid that might become a bore," she said finally.

This remark annoyed him even more. "I'll try to keep you interested," he said shortly.

She placed a hand over his. "I didn't mean that. You're real delicious, Edward, but you're a man. You can go and come at your own whim. I love the touch of you, I love your love. I love the closeness we have and the joy we make, but sitting around an apartment waiting for you is not my idea of living. You forget I'm just eighteen. I'm too energetic to sit and wait."

"You're eighteen," he agreed. "I can see that. Still it's hard for me to believe. You're a new deal in precocity. You speak too well, you've read too much. You're ten years ahead of your age."

She grinned like a vixen. "I'm smart, too. Did I ever tell you about my I. Q.?"

"No. You didn't have to. A bartender in West Falls did, though. Now listen to what I have to say. You put up in the apartment. I'll give you a fistful of green and you get about and shop for what you need…on your own. That'll keep you occupied for a while. Then after you've set your feet good, we'll talk about work. A deal?"

She kissed him explosively in his ear. "That's a deal, Edward."

CHAPTER FOUR

For a week she was happy. She examined the great city, she bought clothes, she walked and walked and walked. Each day she returned to the apartment tired but happy. She would greet him with a flying leap and a hot twisting kiss that often prevented them from moving very far from where contact was first made, but the carpet was soft and deep and it received them gently.

She stretched upon him at full length, her hands crossed on his chest, her firm breasts digging softly into his skin. "Gee, but I had fun today," she said. "So much fun that I ran home and wrote a short story. Is the typewriter your aunt's?"

"Yes. So you wrote a story?"

"Sure. A real good one ... I think. I think I'll try to sell it."

He took her mouth in his and forgot about the story ... and for the second time in a week tears stung his eyes and his chest felt constricted and tight. Edward Carlton was in love and like a man of his type, didn't realize it.

They lived and loved and had great fun but as she predicted, finally came boredom.

She was grateful to him for all he had done for her, so she put off the mention of it for two weeks and to keep herself occupied, wrote furiously. Story after story leaped from the typewriter. She wrote them easily with great speed Plot followed plot without her thinking of them as plots. Story after story took form and such was the lack of consciousness while writing, that often when she re-read for corrections it was like reading something written by someone else. Quite often she'd become excited and her fabulous skin … she wrote in the nude, almost all the time … would become pebbled with gooseflesh. Occasionally she'd gasp with something like shock at some subconscious flight that would appear on the paper. "Did I do that?" she'd ask herself.

Inevitably she became bored even with writing. so she stacked her stories and began to hunt for entertainment.

They lay on the bed in the dimmed room late one night when suddenly she sat up. He started and raised on one elbow. "What's the matter?"

"I've got to have something to do, Colt." It was a nickname she'd coined and he didn't like it. To him it connoted a stallion not yet arrived and this was a sore point.

"I wish you'd stop that," he said crabbily. "What do you want to do?"

"You mentioned modeling."

"Yes. I have a friend who has an agency. We'll see him tomorrow."

He changed his mind in the morning and instead of accompanying her sent her to the address with a note addressed to a Mr. Daniel Larsen who was a thick-shouldered blonde of Norwegian extraction with white lashes and brows and cold green eyes.

He looked at the note, then at her, and licked lips that had suddenly gone dry. "The wonder of the matter is that you got to see me at all. I have a reputation for being hard to see."

She smiled. "May I sit down?"

"Oh … by all means. I'm sorry to seem rude. Matter of fact is, I am rude. I find it no end helpful in my business."

"Another first for me? Maybe the note helped."

He dropped it pointedly into a wastebasket. "Believe me, the note is trash. I know Colton very casually. I know nothing good about him. I hope I don't offend you."

"You don't. I came to see about a job."

He leaned forward. "I'd love to make a model out of you."

"Oh ... thank you."

"Don't thank me. You'll never be a model."

"But you said ..."

"I know what I said. I said I'd love to make one of you and of course I can. I can do anything in the modeling business I want to." He stopped and frowned. "That isn't quite true. I can't make a model look like a woman. That's your trouble. No one on earth could think of you as anything but a woman. It is fatal to look like a woman in this business." He looked at her critically and she felt suddenly deliciously warm and agitated. She liked the cold intenseness of the green eyes and the clean bulk of his body. His lips should have been thin and severe but they were full and sensual.

"I thought all your models were women."

He laughed harshly. "Let us say they are female. There is a vast difference. Didn't you see any as you came in?"

"Yes ... that is, I suppose that's what they were. They looked pretty done up and artificial to me."

"Exactly. Done up and artificial. Take away their artifice and I'd fire the lot. Did you ever see an unretouched photograph of a model?"

"No."

"Now don't get me all wrong. There are beautiful models, but they are the exception or maybe I'm too exacting in my standards." He opened his desk drawer, took out a slick photograph and handed it to her. "She was a brave woman to have that made. Only the very best should attempt nudes."

Marvelle gasped. "Why ... she's sick. There're lines in her face and her ..." She stopped and flushed.

"Yes. You can count her ribs, her pelvic bones are all angles and her breasts are fried eggs with pepper corns on top. Yet she's a good model for certain things. Not lingerie, bras or anything like that. You see, a model strikes the buying female public in two ways. The fat ones sigh for the slim lines and the cute plump ones giggle and tell themselves that they certainly look better than *that*... and they're right. The great value of the modem model is that women, a certain strata of them, are stupid enough to dress for each other rather than men." He looked at his watch. "I'm giving you entirely too much time. My time is as valuable as blue ribbon stock."

"I'm sorry... I ..."

He waved her down. "I'm enjoying it. You intrigue me and even I eat. Will you have lunch with me?"

"I'd love it. But about the job ...

"We'll talk about it."

At Sardis they dined well and Mr. Larsen took more of his valuable time, a matter he was honest to admit had much to do with the girl across the table from him.

"Now," he said as he finished his dessert, "about that job. Must you have one?"

She lifted a thick coppery eyebrow at him. "Isn't that a rather peculiar question?"

His face was neither hard nor soft. "My dear, I happen to know Edward Colton. Your clothes are new and you are quite obviously small town. If that sounds smug, I'm sorry. It's nothing against you, surely, but you're just not big city."

Her eyes met his squarely. "All right. I want a job to keep from being bored to death."

"I'll give you a job if you can sweep, dust, file, type... anything but model."

"Why couldn't I diet and get in shape for a model? Why couldn't I learn?"

"You could do all of that. Do you have a burning ambition to model?"

"No."

"So I thought, and what you'd have to go through wouldn't be worth it." He frowned. "You're having an extraordinary effect on me. That dress...it's so utterly simple and it fits so smoothly, yet not tightly. What were you thinking about when you bought it?"

"Nothing except that I liked it."

"You didn't ponder and wonder and feel it and...oh, hell, all the things women usually do when they choose a dress?"

"No. I think the fitting and purchase might have taken fifteen minutes."

He nodded. "That's what I mean. You must never lose doing things through instinct. Instinct is never wrong. Volition often is."

"What's this I do to you?"

"You've done it to enough men in your time probably. You take possession of my mind. The instant you mentioned modeling I rose up in automatic revolt. It's something that shouldn't happen to your body...to your mind. I get the shakes that something might happen to change that. When do you want to start to work?"

"As soon as possible."

"Very well. Let's go."

She was put to work as Larsen's personal flunky. She filed, she typed and did a hundred things for him that his busy secretary was glad to shift to her shoulders. Her salary shocked her so she mentioned it to him.

"I don't think this is right," she said accusingly, fluttering the check at him.

"You want a raise already?"

She sat suddenly and lifted her liquid violet eyes to his. "You know better than that. It's too much. How many of your help get a hundred a week to start?"

"None."

"Then...?"

"Look at the check."

She looked.

"You'll notice it is not drawn on the firm. It's my personal check. It was mailed to you. None of the others are."

"Mr. Larsen, what does that mean?'"

"It means you lend so damn much to the place that I think you're worth more than you're being paid."

"All I do is file a little, type a little, and run errands."

He grinned. "Maybe its personal. Maybe I feel I'm so important to the firm that anyone or anything that makes me feel better, makes me happier is important to the firm."

She smiled slowly and he almost wriggled. "That's a very nice thing to say," she murmured.

"Sure. I'm full of them."

"Isn't there something I can do for you? I mean…" She blushed a little. "Well… isn't there?"

"There is," he said, suddenly sober. "You can leave Colton's apartment and move into mine."

Her eyes did not change in the slightest. "When shall I move in?"

He was taken aback for a moment. "Just like that?"

He dropped his hands flat on the desk. "What'll I do when you pull up and leave me?"

"If I move in, I reserve the privilege of moving out… just like that."

"All right. I'll take it on that basis." His jaw hardened. "Maybe I'll enjoy the memory. Just thinking of what it was like when you were with me."

"Are you always so pessimistic? The moment I agree to move in your mind leaps to when I might move out."

"I'm not usually pessimistic. The thought just struck me and it was no small blow. Marvelle, I think I know what it'll be like."

She smiled and stood. "I doubt it. When shall I move in?"

"Tonight too soon?"

"No. Tonight will be fine."

She'd hoped to avoid Edward while moving but he walked in and caught her packing.

"What the hell is this?" he asked almost in panic.

"I'm moving," she said crisply and kept at her packing.

"But why?"

"Because I want to."

"After all I've done for you ... bringing you out of the sticks, putting you up in a nice apartment, buying you clothes ..."

"I gave you a few things," She said pointedly. "I've never said no to you on anything yet ... until now, that is. You figure what your outlay was and I'll repay it to the last cent."

"It's not that, and you know it," he said bitterly. "To hell with the money. Marv I want you to stay."

"Nope."

"Where will you go?"

"To Mr. Larsen's apartment."

"That son of a bitch. So that's it."

"That's it. Why is he any more of one than you?"

"I don't feel logical this evening," he said harshly. "I just don't want you to go. What do you want that I haven't given you?"

"It isn't material things, Colt. I'm just bored with you, that's all."

He became frantic and talked shrilly and childishly. He allowed grief to throttle him and he talked thickly through tears. Finally he made the supreme sacrifice.

"I'll marry you," he yelled distractedly.

This shook her more than any of his antics and she blinked twice. "*Marry* me?"

"That's what I said," he lashed at her, his heart sinking at what he'd said, but he knew that if it took marriage to keep her, he'd have to do it.

"Thanks, Colt, but if you bore me now, think how unspeakable it would be married to you. I'm sorry and I do appreciate what you've done for me."

She left him stunned and pale, seated in a chair, his hands hanging limply over his knees.

Later that evening, after her things had been put away in his apartment, considerably lusher than Colton's aunt's place, Marvelle and Larsen went out to dinner. He seemed nervous and though he had helped her with her unpacking, he hadn't attempted to kiss or touch her. She was a little amused and not a little flattered by his attitude.

"I'm afraid the great Mr. Larsen is still a little boy."

Dan Larsen was a very sharp man. He lived in the midst of advertising, show business and publishing. She did not have to draw a picture for him. She was aware of his perturbation.

He blushed furiously. "Was that necessary?" he asked sharply.

She laughed. "Please don't be sensitive, Dan," she said, her voice so soft that he felt all melty inside. "Shall we go?" she asked when he didn't answer.

At the apartment he had his actions under control but his nerves were jumping. He knew very well why he was nervous. She had made no pretense that she was anything but herself. She hadn't played coy about her relationship with Colton. He was afraid that she might turn out a wee bit hard and objective, this siting ill with her loveliness and the evanescent thing that made her glow like a subdued light...her unconquerable youth perhaps might sour him. He had a very short temper with deviousness, but at the same time he had a brightly polished sense of good taste.

She sat on the broad couch that was upholstered in tan nubby silk and said, "Will you build us a couple of drinks, Dan?'"

He did and they drank in silence with Larsen staring moodily at the deep carpet, smoking.

"Maybe we'd better talk," she said stretching her arm to put her finished drink on the glass-topped coffee table supported by curly wrought iron legs.

"Maybe so," he agreed then lapsed into silence again.

She leaned toward him. "This is a side of you I wasn't aware of until today."

He nodded and sighed. "I guess you're right. I'm still a little boy. I'm afraid."

"Of what?"

He shrugged. He couldn't tell her. "I told you you'd taken possession of my mind. I don't think I knew how much until you started reading it. Maybe you can tell me."

She placed a soft hand on his shoulder. "Maybe I can. If I don't, it's because a great compliment to me is involved."

He looked at her in amazement. "This mind reading act isn't funny anymore."

"Want me to stop it?"

"Yes. Please do."

"All right." She went into his arms and the touch of her lips on his made him forget his nervousness as she had known it would.

Dan Larsen was a man of great talent and that night he discovered that he had an even greater talent, that of performing with no conscious thought on the matter at all. Other men had discovered the same thing, but he was probably more impressed. He realized that it had been her fault entirely. They played a duet, she a note and he a note, and since they were in perfect tune, each played the only note that fitted the composition at that moment and the production was perfect.

After the first heated kiss, she got up. "I need a bath, Dan. I worked all day. Wait while I make myself sweet for you."

He too had worked all day and if there was a hint involved, he took it, and when she was through he, too, took a shower. She stood in the door to the bedroom when he emerged clad in a crimson silk robe. She was attired in a light blue robe of satin that clung to her rich curves with the proper respect and when he saw her he didn't stop walking until she was in his arms. His blood roared and pounded in his ears as his hands skidded the rich material over richer skin.

She withdrew to breathe and he could read her thought ... that the bedroom was best for this and if he didn't take the lead he should ... and he did.

She was a slippery succulent fruit and her body was possessed of such voluptuous witchery that a kind of frenzy possessed Larsen. He was no longer the crisp hard executive. He was a youth with a youth's eternal fire, eagerness and impatience. He took her ... or properly, they took each other, because Marvelle was no woman to be left out of such a situation. She received him ... allowed him her mystery of mysteries and inundated him with sweetness, beat him with eagerness, bruised him with the muscular wonder of her body and slaughtered him with reward.

She allowed him to relax but she refused to let him go, holding him with gentle firmness, gobbling up sensations that fled between them, activating others until they were like an electric motor in the grip of wildly active impulses.

With a groan of unendurable want, he crushed her in his arms again and the night began to lose reality to him. He couldn't get enough of her and in the frenzy of seeking, he performed as he never had in his life. She allowed it, her nerves knotted and ragged from the furious onslaught of an emotion and sensation she had never experienced before. It was only the beginning of new things he taught her while he learned because Daniel Larsen had never been put in a position before where everything seemed right and everything proper.

He had begged her forgiveness afterward. " I hope ... it was all right with you."

She clutched his head between her breast and became so overcome that she wept. She had become emotionally involved for the first time and it was the beginning of her downfall. It was while she was involved with Larsen that she began to drink seriously. In the months that followed her moving to his apartment, they were inseparable Day was merely a prelude to night and night was a sensual Bacchanal There seemed no end to their desire and their versatility made it last. When they were certain that everything had been discovered, they found excitement in rediscovery.

She found a wantonness in her behavior when she was feeling alcohol that released her for the ultimate in enjoyment of her senses. To Larsen, who couldn't drink much, this was a revelation and soul food, food he had been sorely needing all his mature life.

But boredom, the nemesis that was to dog her relentlessly for a long time, began to rear its head and she drank more. She felt certain that she was in love with him and couldn't bear the thought of leaving him, but even this paled in time and soon they stood at their crossroads. There had been a huge party of advertisers at an executive's plush home in Westchester. Larsen and Marvelle attended, whereupon Marvelle became steaming drunk as did Mr. Walter Campbell, the lingerie king.

They were discovered on a little glassed-in side porch at two the next morning, both nude, both passed out.

Larsen went home alone in a steaming fury, sick with disgust and so emotionally brutalized that he couldn't go to the office next day. This was a shock because the agency was his life and he knew something would have to be done.

She came in a cab in time to drink a glass of orange juice and fall exhausted into bed where she couldn't sleep. She got up and started drinking all over again. They had several terrific rows during which neither was quite rational or reasonable but both passionately devoted to their pet theme of the moment.

"I tell you I didn't know what I was doing," she said tearfully. "I got drunk and it happened. I don't like him. I never did and I still don't."

"No one made you drink," he reminded her cuttingly.

"You ought to try it yourself," she retorted heatedly. "Maybe you'd discover you were a human being."

"I can't take it and I know it," he shot back. "You can't and won't admit it. You'll go on drinking and end up a slattern, an alcoholic who'll sell herself for a drink. Thanks, I don't care for any."

It went on like that for the most of the day until he, in a fresh burst of rage, left the apartment and hard on his heels, she left, too. She rented a small place near Central Park and it was a week before he, through the offices of a private detective, found her.

"I want to see you," he said quietly over the phone.

"How did you find me?" she wanted to know.

"That's not important," he said. "May I come out?"

"Yes. I owe you that, but I'll tell you one thing. You have become a bore and I don't want to see you. I absolutely and finally will not come back so you'll be wasting your time. Just the same, I'll see you if you want."

"I'll be out in thirty minutes."

Daniel Larsen had a good solid mind and proved it when he was almost out of the cab in front of her apartment house. "Just a moment, driver." He got back in. "I've changed my mind."

"Sure," said the driver knowingly. "Most of em ain't worth it anyhow."

"I said I had changed my mind. I didn't offer to share it."

"Okay by me, bud," said the driver and eased into Broadway traffic from Sixty-Fourth Street.

Marvelle continued her binge after moving and was discovered by her maid one morning in bad shape. She was shipped off to Bellevue after the police were called by the maid who thought she was dead.

CHAPTER FIVE

A kindly psychiatrist spoke to her briefly. "Miss Martingale, you're an unusual alcoholic…"

She sat up in her bed instantly. "What do you mean, alcoholic? I'm no such thing. I just had a little too much that was all. My maid caused all this hurrah by calling the police."

The doctor smiled and looked at the chart attached to a clipboard. He tilted it toward her. "The maid stated you'd been drunk for a week."

Marvelle opened her mouth to call the girl a liar, but stopped. She was a basically honest person and not even in self-defense could she do it. She slumped a little. "I'd been drinking before she knew anything about it… but I'm not an alcoholic."

The doctor sighed. "You're typical, Miss Martingale. Few alcoholics will admit to their condition. It makes our work a great deal harder. We're fearfully overloaded here. We don't have the time to give each patient. My approach was designed to see if you fitted into the pattern. In private practice, I'd have been more diplomatic. You fit and until you can knuckle under, admit that you're an alcoholic, admit that you've a problem you can't handle alone, I'm afraid I can't do much for you."

"All right," she said harshly. "Suppose I admit it. What then?"

"First, you aren't admitting it. You're still resentful and you haven't admitted it to yourself. However, I will tell you that in the event you sincerely wanted help, I'd first try to discover, if possible, what caused you to lean on alcohol. I'd try to explain it as clearly as possible to you so you could grasp it completely. In the event that we discovered what the cause was, we'd still have taken but a feeble step. Alcoholism is a combination of things, among which are problems of physical addiction which you are approaching, but I fear already have reached. The bare knowledge of the predisposing cause is a help only in that we just *might* correct it. The physical addiction would still have to be cured but I will say that once the cause is corrected, the cure is a lot easier and you would be less likely to return to the state."

She frowned. "You don't sound much like a psychiatrist. You make sense."

He laughed. "It sounds like you've been occupying a couch."

"I could take that two ways," she replied. "I suppose you mean I've been to a psychoanalyst?"

"Yes."

"No. I read a lot and I've read about them. I don't think I could go for what they hand out."

"There is some objection to their methods," he admitted carefully. "Well, Miss Martingale, I regret that I don't have time to talk further with you. You seem intelligent and you are undeniably beautiful. Please, for your own sake, don't abuse this beauty with a bottle." He handed her a card. "My own time is taken up here at the hospital, but if you are ever in need of the very best professional help, Dr. Leibermann is a good friend of mine, just out of his residency and anxious for patients. He was a general practitioner and a gynecologist before he became a psychiatrist. He won't offend your sense of logic with couch sessions. He'll talk to you, advise you and do his best to help.'"

She took the card. "I won't need him," she said with finality.

"Yes," he said sadly. "You really think you won't... but you will."

Marvelle, back home from her nerve-wracking visit to an alcoholic ward in the biggest hospital in the world, reached almost automatically for a drink. With glass in hand, she sat in a deep comfortable chair... looked at the drink and put it down carefully. Then for the first time in her life she forced herself to take stock. The drinking habit had come down on her suddenly. She was honest enough and fundamental enough to realize that it had happened while she was living with Larsen. Pursuing introspection further, she realized that another first had been emotional involvement with what had in the past been almost purely physical. She realized that in the absorption with sex, there had, in play and in act, been considerable emotional quotient but it was satisfied in the same manner and at the same time that physical hunger was assuaged. There had been no emotional hangover or residue to plague her. With Larsen and his total abandonment to the pipes of pan had come a similar response from her that had unstoppered the evil vial and loosed the eroding torments of love.

She got up abruptly and took a cold tinging shower. She burnished her skin with a towel and right upon the heels of this mild symbolic flagellation came a ripping quake of want so sharp and shaking that she had to lean against the wall of the bathroom to recover.

She went to the living room and sprawled nude on the couch. It was a mistake. The torment grew. Her skin became acutely sensitive and every move sent sheets of desire roaring over her in a hot wet flood. She sat up and with a gesture of finality picked up the drink and drained it in a few gulps. Instantly it seemed the fiery burn began to tingle her system and she relaxed a little. Her nerves, not yet dulled by the drink, began to torment her and she began to pace up and down. The more she paced the worse it became until out of sheer desperation she called a typewriter agency and ordered a rental machine to be delivered.

While she waited impatiently she poured another bourbon and water and drank it slower and thought. That she was really becoming or had reached the state of an alcoholic, her vanity would not allow her to admit but there was one thing certain, she would have to get another job. She had saved money because she had had little upon which to spend it, but it would not last forever.

It was in this thoughtful mood that she put on a robe when she heard the doorbell ring, admitted the slim fresh-cheeked lad with the typewriter and ushered him out without reacting to the fact that he was young, personable, with hot roving eyes and that she needed such a man desperately.

When she did think about it, she used some very unlady-like words and ran a sheet of paper into the machine. She typed with nervous surcharged fury and the story poured out with her scarcely conscious of what she was writing. She felt a strange exhilaration when she was done. She was relaxed and rather tired. More than that, she was hungry, so she dressed and went out to dinner.

At dinner she saw Maxine Loren come in with a young man on her arm so she waved them to her table. Maxine was the severely lanky receptionist at Larsen Associates and Maxine liked her.

"Well," said the carefully rigged ex-model as she allowed her escort to seat her. "What's with you and job and boss and what-not? Oh ... Marvelle, this is Hugo Winters. He's with lingerie and Rosenbloom and Company."

Winters was short, round and balding with protruding fishy eyes that roved suggestively. At the moment they were bugged considerably beyond their usual limits. Marvelle, dressed in a powder blue knit creation, was contributing not a little to his avid gaze.

"Now," said Maxine, "as I was saying ..."

"Just a disagreement," replied Marvelle shortly. "We don't see eye to eye anymore."

"Well, I wish something would happen to return the eyes to agreement. Dan's a bear. He's normally hard to live with ... genius, you know. At the present tie's impossible."

"Disagreement." Winters nodded and eyed her boldly. "That one word is a really fabulous linguistic compression. A distillate, as it were. I'll have to speak to our advertisers about it. If they work on it, they might come up with something as potent as walking a mile for Burpo soda."

Maxine cut him with a withering glance. "You'd sell drawers at your mother's funeral."

"I eat, live and breathe drawers," he said with a giggle. "Although at the moment I want something like a big steak running red with all the trimmings.

"A steak," Marvelle heard herself saying, "doesn't run red with trimmings. Blood does it."

Winters giggled and took his eyes from the low neckline of her dress with an effort. "So it does. I'm not an advertising man. Words throw me."

"That's because you have lingual diarrhea, darling," said Maxine, her sharp angular face cut with lines of distaste and the effects of time. "We're going to Waldo Penticost's place after dinner, Marvelle. Wouldn't you like to go along?"

Marvelle's breath quickened. Penticost's parties were reputed to develop into orgies more often than not. They were a haven for jaded socialites, show people and freeloaders. She had heard that some weird things often happened there.

"I think I'd like that. Would he mind?"

"Mind squeaked Winters shrilly. "He'd murder us if he knew we had left something like you to go to a show or home to bed."

Penticost's apartment was a penthouse atop the Marblehead Hotel and Marvelle wondered what his rent was what with the kind of place it was and the service Penticost, a fabulously successful lawyer, demanded. The party was in full swing as they ushered in and Marvelle could see that New York was well represented. She saw models with whom she had a nodding acquaintance, photographers she had seen at Larsen Associates, upper echelon men of the publishing world of whom she had heard, actresses, club performers and the sickly, pale Bleakely who had drawn patrons in droves for three years to an obscure night spot in the Village, had huddled with an enormous Chickering at one end of the living room and the air tinkled with her magnificent improvisations. Some of the guests, those who had skipped dinner and those to whom alcohol was a mild poison, had already started to stagger and paw. Someone thrust a drink into her hands and a cool moist hand caught her arm and directed her to a small couch in a corner.

"I'm Rufe Grotewald," said the fat little man whose eyes were already glazed. His bald spot shone like a full moon, his lips were loose and wet and his hands repulsive.

"I'm in TV advertising. When you're not the loveliest thing at a party, what do you do?"

Marvelle was repelled and angry. She was not in a good mood and the cool sting of the drink on her stomach, instead of mellowing her, made her belligerent.

"I'm queer," she said distinctly.

"Oh…" He simpered and licked his lips. One eyelid dropped suggestively. "Well…there are things that may be said for the fault. I'm not a stickler for heterogony myself. What particular form does your peculiarity take?"

"I was reared on a farm," she said. "I like animals." She discovered that he was shock proof.

He giggled again. "You don't say. Well, you have company. See the big girl in the slinky black dress? So's she. She keeps a regular kennel."

It was Marvelle who was shocked but she managed not to show it. "Really, I must talk to her."

"Oh she's a card all right. I've seen it."

She felt herself going pale. "Seen it?"

"Oh sure. She likes to make a circus out of it."

Marvelle got up abruptly and with a quick sinuous movement lost herself from him in the crowd. She acquired another drink and after drinking it began to soar. She found herself pushed up against a man and looked up. Although she was tall for a girl, this man loomed over her. She guessed his height at six-three and he was the lean, tanned, outdoorsy type.

"Sorry," she said. "I'm trying out for the Giants. Linebacker."

He gave her a slow lazy smile that made her tingle so heatedly that the end result was weakening.

"I'll get you a tryout. I'm Craine Frazer."

"I'm Marvelle Martingale. How did we get here?"

"I was dragged. Now I wish I had the guts to drag myself away… but these sort of gatherings fascinate me in the way a rattler fascinates a bird."

"I was dragged, too. I was just shocked to the wisdom teeth by a man… I use the word gingerly, whom *I* was trying to shock. Poetic justice, in a manner of speaking."

Sound swirled around them and gave her a chance to digest what her eyes had gathered.

She raised her eyes. "Texas?"

"Midland," he said with a smile. "I suppose my boots gave me away."

"Yes. Why do you wear them?"

"What's wrong with them aside from the fact that few people wear them?"

"Just that. Boots in New York."

"I never wore anything else. I tried and felt like I was standing in a hole. I have temperamental feet. I decided I'd rather be conspicuous than uncomfortable."

She laughed. "I'm for it. You're a breath of fresh air in this smog."

"You," he said with sober gallantry, "are a breath of fresh air where there's nothing but fresh air. Miss Martingale, I think you're probably the most beautiful woman I ever saw."

She was startled, not by the remark because that had become almost commonplace, but she recognized sincerity when she heard it.

She raised her great eyes to his and for a long moment held them. "Thank you, Mr. Frazer. I appreciate that...really."

It was his turn to be startled and by much the same thing. She seemed almost pathetically grateful for a remark he was sure she had heard many times before.

A group of surging people barged between them and she lost him. Bleakley stood before her catching her searching eyes.

"Ah...a Circe among us. I could compose a classic to such beauty."

Her first reaction was one of anger. The next reaction was, she realized, the cause of it and probably deserved first place. His flowery greeting sounded as false as a lead coin compared with Frazer's calm compliment. She forced a smile. "Your beauty is in your hands. Will you play for me?"

"If you'll help me blaze a trail to the piano. I shall also require that you hang yourself over my shoulder and pay rapt attention."

"Girdle indeed. I don't wear *anything*," snarled a scratchy voice at their right. They looked. She was a tall willowy blonde who was very drunk. "They're for such frumps as you, darling. I'll show you." She did and she proved her point.

Bleakley caught Marvelle's arm and swung her about. "A drunk woman is an anathema," she growled in his falsetto. "A drunken woman without a shred of decency or taste is worse than a garbage probing dog. Let's see if I can erase that sordid scene from your mind."

His magic fingers raced over the keyboard. She listened entranced for a time and drank three more drinks.

After the last drinks the night began to haze for the girl and she could never recall leaving Bleakley and the piano. She drifted about, seldom going very far before some man pounced and began to breathe heavily. There were a succession of them, all drunk, all with the same proposition, some propositions fancier than others. Some oblique or subtle, others a flat bold request and at least three didn't seem to realize that others were present or didn't care. After several more drinks. she discovered an institution known as "behind the potted plant." a lush well-tended shrub that obscured an alcove from the guests. The first visitor she saw emerge was the tall willowy blonde whose lipstick had been bountifully smeared and whose dress front seemed a little bent and askew. Her skirt, of some traitorous synthetic material, clung to her waist on one side and didn't fall until she had taken several steps from the protection of the shrub.

She had more drinks and before her fuddled mind could quite encompass what was transpiring, she found herself behind the plant shoved against a cute contrivance that allowed her to stand and yet lean back at a severe angle. Her male accomplice was none other than her earlier friend, the TV advertising executive, Grotewald, whose hands, abetted by her alcoholic weakness and the abnormal heat it had generated, found themselves occupied. She clutched him … his lips found hers and for a passion-fraught minute she became a hungry animal seeking what was her. The night became mad and violent and the host, feeling that he now had the proper grist for his show, touched a hidden button and the potted plant slid smoothly aside and revealed the performers, who not knowing that they were revealed, continued their little drama. Marvelle, mercifully, couldn't stand the combined action of the drinks she had consumed and the racketing shock of physical reaction that affected her like a bolt of blasting lightning. With a cry, she slid to the floor, out cold.

CHAPTER SIX

When Marvelle woke up, bright sunlight was filtering through Venetian blinds into her eyes. With a groan she rolled over and went into a semi-coma for a while. She was accustomed to sleeping nude and it was the scrounging of pajamas big enough for two of her that finally brought her back to the world of reality.

Degree by painful degree she returned to the land of the living and managed to sit up in an unbalanced sort of way. She was in a strange, lovely apartment done in the softest pastels with comfortable furniture, matching or harmonizing with the decor. The bed was somewhat smaller than a handball court but the sheets were plain white percale. There were several mannish paintings on the walls and one excellent Remington lithograph depicting a western scene. Something about the mannishness of the pictures and the suave appointments of the apartment clashed but it was a nuance she was not capable of registering at the moment.

Sitting up had been a mistake because her stomach, which had been sort of a gone void vaguely attached to her middle, now woke up and struck with the savagery of a rattler. She tumbled out of bed and found the bathroom after the third try, barely making it in time. She was violently ill for a long time, retching with such heroic energy that she was soon drenched with sweat and limp with weakness. She sank to the floor to her knees, then to sitting and nearly went blind with a fresh fury of emesis.

"Now ain't you a fine sight," trumped a brazen female voice but Marvelle was too ill and weak to even look around. She emitted a hollow groan and clung to the toilet bowl to keep from keeling over.

Again she strove to vomit and things grew grey then black but she still had consciousness enough to feel strong hands that caught her, picked her up like a feather pillow and carried her back to bed. Her stomach was in convulsions...heaving and jerking against her will. Then came icy cloths for her throat and forehead and a sense of falling delightfully into a bottomless pit of comfort. Her stomach stopped its wild leaping and she slept. The room was quiet when she woke with only a soporific hum of street noises which she scarcely heard filtering through.

"Well, I told myself you'd live. Looks like you'll make it."

She stared and turned her head toward the doorway leading to the living room and saw framed in it a giantess as black as coal with a huge jolly moonface, a large grinning mouth decorated by teeth that seemed glaring white in the black face. She was fat but her fatness was only an addition to a tremendous frame. She walked on in with a hard fast stride. "Gal, you was *some* sick this mornin'."

Marvelle essayed a smile that she hoped wasn't too much of a travesty. "You can say that again. Where am I?"

The woman erupted into a trumpet of a laugh. "He said you wouldn't remember comin' here. Tole me to watch you careful like so's you wouldn't jump out of a window or nuthin."

"I'm Marvelle Martingale. Who're you and who's he?"

"My name's Amanda Thornhill Johnston and if you call me 'Mandy,' you won't *hafta* jump outa the window and my boss is Mr. Frazer. He brung you home las' night...more this mornin' it was.

Marvelle searched her fuddled mind for a man named Frazer but came up with nothing. Fragments of the party came back to her even to the point of going behind the potted plant and some of what went on ... then nothing. She shuddered and began to feel nausea again.

"Here now," said Amanda sitting on the bed. "Don't start that. He'll come home and think I been beatin' you." "Now what's it all about, honey. You can tell ole Amanda about it.

She cuddled against the big warm body and sobbed out the story of last night in such vehement detail.

Amanda heard her out then stroked her hair into place drinkin'. It's just plain poison to some people. My third husband could take two drinks and fall down a long flight of stairs. I've seen Mr. Frazer drink all day and all night and never get drunk. Some can, some can't. You didn't smoke no tea or sniff no snow, did you?"

"Oh ... no. That's dope."

"So's whiskey to some."

She dropped her face in her hands. "How on earth will I face him? What will I do?"

Amanda patted her shoulder. "Now don't you worry none about that. He ain't no preacher and he ain't none of your kin and he's the best man ever come outa the state of Texas and that's where *men* come from, honey. Take it from me who knows."

"Texas ... does he wear boots?"

"Sure. Got more boots'n I got shoes. That man do love boots."

It came back to her then and she lay back in silent agony. The one really impressive man in the whole mass of people and he should be the one to see her shame and to hold out a helping hand. It was too much to bear.

"Now," said Amanda getting up, "I'm gonna go 'long with you to the bathroom. You gonna brush your teeth, take a bath and get inter some slacks and a sweater he had sent up. Your pretty jersey dress was ruint ... what with one thing and another. He'll be home in a hour or so and you want to look plumb right for him."

This was incentive enough to get her out of bed and in thirty minutes she not only looked different but felt as though she might live. The slacks were a little small but on Marvelle the effect was wonderful. The sweater, also a little small, produced an effect that made Amanda whistle at her. "Gal, you sure look fitten right now. Them things is a little small but I always say when you got it, a tight fit don't do nuthin' but light the Christmas tree. If you got it, don't be afraid to show it off. Now...Mr. Frazer always likes breakfast, don't make no difference what time of day he gets up. You name it, I'll fix it."

The thought of food made her realize that of late she hadn't been eating enough and now she was hungry. She smiled. "Breakfast would be fine, Amanda and I hope you make good coffee."

"If you're used to yankee coffee, mine'll get you drunk all over again. I makes coffee to wake the dead, honey."

It was not long before Marvelle, who hated being waited on, was seated at the kitchen table and watching Amanda whip up a delicious breakfast. There were eggs scrambled with cream and a dash of Tabasco, cooked in yellow butter, thin slices of sour misch bread and butter toasted delicately and crisply and a hefty ham steak that was the most delicious Marvelle had ever tasted. She ate heartily and washed it down with steaming black coffee that was a sharp biting shock at first but the rich winey bite began to tickle her taste and by the time the first cup was finished, she was ready to try the second.

Amanda sat with her and drank a cup of coffee while she ate, watching with pleasure her evident enjoyment of the breakfast. She eyed the girl critically. "Honey, you're sure figured up to please, but please don't go on with this drinkin'. It'll ruin you sure and you won't be nuthin' but a shadder with your pretty face all wrinkled up and dried out."

"I can handle it," said Marvelle with a flash of belligerence.

"You sure wasn't handlin' it last night."

"It slipped up on me."

"That can happen. How many more times is it slipped up on you?"

She was kept from answering this embarrassing question by the door to the corridor opening. Frazer stepped in and stood for a moment looking at them through the kitchen door.

His face was reposed, serious and Marvelle thought, disapproving. "Afternoon," he said softly.

Amanda got up. "Coffee's ready. Come set down. She decided not to die on us but she tried hard."

He came and sat at the table, one corner of his mouth curving in a half smile softening what she had taken for disapproval. Her heart was in her feet and she couldn't speak.

"You seem in better shape right now," he said.

Amanda poured him a cup of coffee and effaced herself. He sweetened the coffee and sipped it, then lit a long dark-paper cigarette of a kind Marvelle had never seen before. It had a rich, cigarry bouquet.

She could stand it no longer. "All right, say it and get it over with ... and I am grateful to you for taking care of me."

He looked fixedly into his coffee and tapped ash from the cigarette with a long forefinger. "Someone had to," he said in his habitually gentle voice. "There was a trick to the potted plant love nest, it seems. Our host, besides knowing a lot of peculiar people, also has a rather unsanitary sense of humor. He didn't pull the pin on the others but when you and your friend went behind the bush, he rolled it aside ... electronically, I suppose, but there you were."

She went as pale as chalk and a trembling hand went to her mouth. "Oh *no* ..."

"Yes. Your friend seemed to think that the world had fallen on him when he finally realized that the performance was public."

She felt the same way now and she put her fingertips to her temples and pressed with all her strength. "Oh no ... Oh no ..."

He was silent until she recovered a little. "Sorry about it," he said at length. "I just didn't have you picked for the type."

"Why did you bother with me?" she said in a dull voice.

"For one thing, I didn't like the atmosphere. For another thing...and I can't quite explain this, the impression you made on me sober was stronger than the one you made when the plant rolled aside. So...I have two impressions so far apart as to constitute war between them. The last and worst was the most graphic and yet it hasn't entirely vanquished the first."

"And that was?"

He shrugged his wide shoulders. "Hard to say because it was something like the thread of perfume you pick out of a crisp morning breeze. Sort of there and not there. Compressed into a pill. I must have told myself, now here is a country girl, fresh, unspoiled, alive. vibrant. eager for life and living, observant and like me, out of her depth in this mess of tainted humanity."

"And you found out differently," she concluded bitterly.

"In a manner of speaking. Still I didn't lose the essential part of the pill. Like I said, there's a battle going on."

"If it's all right with you, I'll take myself out of your sight," she said with desperate resignation. "I know what you think of me and in view of what you saw, I can't offer a word in defense."

"I'm perfectly willing to give you the chance."

"Why?"

"Because of the battle I mentioned. I know I should be completely satisfied that my pill was only a bitter dose fed to me through a beauty that I'd never seen before, a beauty that got me deep down. I had to think several times before I went into that corner and picked you up. Penticost didn't want me to take you. Said he'd bed you down himself and knowing he meant it, I told him to move aside or I'd put you down and break his bones. He moved."

Tears leaked from her eyes now in a steady stream. Her head was bowed in agony. "I'm so ashamed I could die," she said chokingly. I'll leave now and believe me, you'll never know how much a appreciate what you did … especially when you must have hated the very thought of it."

"I was disturbed," he said softly, "but I didn't hate it. I think I was confused. Where will you go?"

"To my apartment."

"Do you need any money?"

"No … *no*."

"Is there anything you need?"

"Yes. I need it from you but I don't deserve it and I lost any chance I had of deserving it last night. Goodbye, Mr. Frazer, and thanks … a whole lot."

They got up and he went to the door with her. "Where do you live?"

"I don't think you'd care to know that. I wouldn't want to see you again because I'd live all over again what happened. I couldn't stand much more of it … knowing how I must disgust you."

"I'm still confused," he said blankly.

"Maybe this'll help. I'm not ashamed of what I did. I'm ashamed I was so far gone that I'd act that way in a crowd … that he moved the bush and …" She turned and ran from the apartment slamming the door behind her.

"That poor chile," said Amanda, her big black eyes glistening with tears.

He turned. "You listened, I suppose."

"You better believe I listened. I took care of her all day and let me tell you, she crawled under my skin like a chigger."

"Then you like her?"

"Sure I likes her."

"What about last night … did she tell you?"

"She tole me and you know what, she didn't try to hide behind *nuthin*. She come right out with it just as plain as brass. If she'da lied, I'da known it."

"That," he said forcefully, "is what has me confused."

"She got under your skin, too, I betcha."

"Yes. No denying of that and yet ..."

"Sure ... what she done behind that brush. troubled about."

"You best forget it. She's gone and New York is a big town."

He sighed deeply. "Yes, I suppose so but, Amanda, she needs someone to lean on."

"She'll find somebody. She'll find somebody who wasn't at that party last night and he'll never know."

She arrived at her apartment, her nerves screeching and her mind as sick as her stomach had been earlier. In despair she sat down at the typewriter and poured out the ache and sickness of her soul until tears blurred the keyboard and the desire for a drink began to nag.

CHAPTER SEVEN

Edward Colton managed to find where she lived and called her. He wept and begged and pleaded until out of sheer nervous desperation she cursed him wildly and hung up. Now, she thought, if Dan Larsen called it would make her day perfect. She grimaced and made herself a drink, drinking it down with driving haste. She felt better immediately, then pondered for a while on her condition.

"I can stop it any time I want to," she said, unconsciously aping countless thousands who had told themselves the same thing. Marvelle's temperament and personality were rather extraverted. She had never thought deeply about motives nor had she ever attempted to coldly and calculatedly examine her deepest drives or to identify them. Some would say that she lacked will power. If she wanted to do something strongly enough, she had generally proceeded as soon after the impulse as was practicable. This attitude explained in a large part the situations in which she found herself all the way from her early capitulation to the efforts of Cannonball Barton, the debacle involving her teacher, Spike Bordelon, the even worse one with Harold Graves, to both the men she had known intimately since coming to New York, and the terrible embarrassment of the Penticost party. Characteristically, the actual performance did not affect her as much as the fact that Craine Frazer, the most impressive man she had ever known, had been a witness.

He couldn't know as she knew that nothing in her had changed, that she was not a hopelessly evil person ... She sat up and caught her breath. What was an evil person? A person who did evil things? Was what she had done evil? She compressed her lips. No. The only thing evil about it was that she had been drunk and in company with a man whom she wouldn't ordinarily have given the time of day. This made her feel better for a moment until she realized that she knew how she felt but *he* didn't.

She took out the card the psychiatrist at Bellevue had given her, looked at it and threw it away with violence, only to leap to her feet and retrieve it immediately. She did not examine the reason for the act, but this time she had to shove the question forcibly from her mind. For a week she wrote, having begun her first attempt at novel writing. During the week she drank every day but with a grim determination not to let it get the best of her. She succeeded in never going off the deep end but the result was probably worse. She stopped eating. She drank milk from her tiny refrigerator, on occasions she'd scramble or soft-boil an egg, but she remembered Amanda's excellent breakfast and felt miserable about her own ... and all the while she drank. Saturday night she decided she owed herself the luxury of a walk and dinner out, so she dressed in a pale blue jersey sheath, put on her coat and left the apartment.

She decided that dinner would taste a lot better if she took the taste of bourbon from her mouth with a few martinis, so she went to a very plush bar a few doors off Broadway on Sixtieth Street. Misjudging how much bourbon she had drunk during the day as well as the potency of the unaccustomed martinis, she was soon ripe for a man of course one appeared. Her memory of what transpired after that was not of the clearest. First there was one man, slim, dapper and rather perfumed, then several more joined them. She had the faintest memory of someone suggesting that they leave the joint and go to his diggings where they could really tie one on ... which apparently was what they did. She recalled in a garbled way that they rode in a cab and that she dispensed her favors lavishly, her kisses starved and ravenous, making no objections to being fondled by one man while kissing another. They made it up to the room and from then on things began to black out for her. She recalled them undressing her and could remember being visited by three different ones and treating them all with wild, furious energy, then the darkness that had been creeping over her brain, was complete.

When she woke it was nearly daylight. Two men were snoring in drunken slumber in two chairs, two others had her boxed tightly between them in the bed. All were nude. Clothes were scattered about like they had been arranged by a strong wind. Her dress was on the floor. It was trodden and dirty. Her bra was thrown carelessly over the back of the couch and only her coat had been hung up ... it on the doorknob with half of it trailing on the floor. She climbed shakily and carefully from the bed, shuddering with mental and physical nausea. Frazer should see her now. Gritting her teeth against weakness and a desire to throw up her insides, she managed to get all her clothes on but her pants. She couldn't find them and when she remembered vaguely that they had been taken off in the cab, she stopped searching and staggered from the room.

On the street, she became weaker and weaker and the nausea that she had been fighting off overcame her.

She remembered vomiting ... on all fours and of people walking around her and finally a policeman asked her name and helped her to her feet. She tried to talk to him but before she could speak, she fainted.

She awakened and found her surroundings familiar.

"Hello," came a familiar voice. "The same girl ... even the same bed in the same ward. The odds against that are great ... that last part, I mean."

She opened her eyes and saw the same psychiatrist who had talked to her before. Tears came to her eyes and she closed them again. He sat by the bed and stroked her hand.

"Feel up to a little yak?"

"I suppose so," she said with weary resignation, "but I'm *not* an alcoholic."

"Not convinced yet?"

"No ... I can quit it any time I wish."

"Then why in God's name don't you?"

She shuddered and swallowed drily. There was no answer to this question.

He got up and patted her shoulder. "Better use that card I gave you. I don't think I can do anything for you in the time I'd have and it's certain you would be of little help. If you can stop drinking, why don't you, or did you enjoy and orgy last night?"

She opened her eyes wide. "What do you know about last night?"

He smiled at her. "Miss Martingale, much can be learned from our lab tests. At least one of the men was infected. You've been given a big prophylactic dose of penicillin which will probably take care of that." He shook his head. "There is something very like sacrilege in a woman as lovely as you letting go like this. You weren't given your beauty for such swinish purposes. If you had one friend or several and they were decent people, I wouldn't say a word, but I think you allowed yourself to get picked up last night and at least four men had a ball with you."

Marvelle wanted to die, she shuddered and began to cry, then went into a flowery convulsion that made the doctor ring for a nurse. He gave rapid orders and sat on the side of the bed and forcibly held her. She pitched and writhed and screamed until the nurse got back. Together they gave her a strong dose of Luminal and as he expected, she quieted long before the drug could have acted. When she was asleep, the doctor left with the nurse.

"Day in and day out," sighed the nurse, a stout, kind-faced, matronly woman. "They never learn, do they?"

"Not nearly often enough," he agreed wearily. "I guess I brought it on, but I was trying to show her what she was doing to herself.

"Yes," agreed the nurse. "Some of them don't even care, much less pitch a fit over it."

On the way back to her apartment the next day, Marvelle seriously considered suicide and the thought frightened her to the core. For the first time she began to realize that things were wrong... very wrong. She took the card from her purse and gave the driver another address.

She realized then that her dress was a sight and she needed a long hot bath, a shampoo and some fresh clothes. Again she redirected the driver who was in too good a mood to get angry with her vacillation and continued his cheery whistling.

For half a day she treated her body with the most loving care and when at last she was ready for the street, she bore little resemblance to the woman in the alcoholic ward.

She wanted a drink until the desire all but overpowered her but she was afraid to touch it. She went to a restaurant and ate slowly and well. After she had eaten, she felt a great deal better and much stronger.

Without a thought of ringing for an appointment or that it was getting late in the afternoon, she took the elevator, in a building on the corner of Broadway and Forty-fifth.

As she got off the elevator she met a tall, striking man walking down the corridor apparently headed for the elevator. He was dark, blue-bearded of the type that can shave three times a day and are still bluebeards, his chin strong and cleft and his eyes a startling blue.

Their eyes met and held and he smiled. "If you're looking for a psychiatrist and one by the name of Aaron Leibermann, just think how close you came to missing me."

She didn't speak, just handed him the card the Bellevue psychiatrist had given her.

He laughed delightedly. "Now isn't that something? I was kidding you because I was certain you weren't coming to see me.

I dared kid you because you are too lovely to pass and say nothing to. Where did you get this?"

"I've been in the alcoholic ward for two days," she said in a subdued voice. "I've been there twice." He inclined his head and his eyes seemed to penetrate her skin, they were so intense.

"That must be Hugh McCoy. We graduated together and took our boards at the same time. He sends me patients. Did you call for an appointment?"

She shrugged helplessly. "I'm afraid not.

He frowned slightly. "I was headed home and very happy about it. I'm about to do something that is foreign to me and I know why I'm doing it, but I don't like it."

"What's that?"

"I'm going to see you even though you had no appointment, even though I am headed home. The reason is because you're such a delight to the eye that I find myself only half believing it. You should be cultivated at all costs and naturally I mean that from a medical standpoint because I am a happily married man with four children. Rosa resents my women patients anyhow. Shall we go back to my lair?"

"I'd appreciate it very much. He gave me this card the first time I went to Bellevue. I'm just now using it, so by that you can conclude that I'm reaching the end of my rope."

"Come along and we'll beat the hell out of this thing. Believe me we will."

She felt better before they reached the office and when finally he had lighted a cigarette for her and she was relaxed he said, "I don't know whether Hugh told you, but I'm a sort of free worker. By that I mean I have my own ideas about psychiatry. Not exclusively, mind you, because I've been impressed that some of the best brains in psychiatry agree with me. I have no couch as you can see, and my method, if it can be so called is that I have faith in the fundamental strength of the human psyche. People become confused and their minds invaded by emotions to the point where they can't think straight, then comes compensation in one of its many forms, the braggarts, the withdrawers, the sadists, the masochists, the seekers of euphoria, the seekers of oblivion ... and so on. From you I ask only that you use your mind and follow me. I do not treat psychotics and I abhor neurotics it they love their neurosis more than they do normalcy. Hypochondriacs are never so happy as when they are discovering or relating the details of some new malady. You're neither a psychotic, a neurotic nor a hypochondriac. What would you say you are, and I'm perfectly serious when I ask this. I have the failing of making snap judgments and I keep at it because I'm so often right. You are a very intelligent young woman. Now what makes you an alcoholic?"

She lifted her shoulders. "I'm not the type. I've had drinks since I was twelve. I enjoyed the sensation, I never got drunk and I never really wanted the stuff. Maybe if I give you a quick history of myself from the time ... oh say when I first realized what a wonderful thing it was to be a woman ..."

"Do so, but I'll ask just one thing. Tell me the truth. You'll know if you've glossed situations over for the benefit of your ego. Don't waste my time showing me Christmas trees. I want the stark naked truth."

She swallowed. "I ... I'll do my best." And she did. She talked for an hour and a half ... until her mouth was dry, but she told him everything as naked and unvarnished as she could make it. She told him of the night before her last visit to the hospital lifelessly, her eyes brimming with tears, and her throat thick with pain, but she didn't miss over a single detail.

"I have some fresh orange juice in my refrigerator," he said when she finished and sank back in her chair. "Would you like some?"

"I'd like some very much. I'm dry."

He came back with tall frosted glasses and they drank a silent toast.

"All right," he said as he handed her a cigarette and extended his lighter. "You've told me the whole thing and be glad that you could come out with matters that must have been like dragging fishhooks through your skin."

"You'll never *know*."

"Yes, I know. I get so weary of people who pay me money, then tell me a pack of palpable lies that I could scream. You were merciless to yourself but honesty, real, shiny steel honesty, is always a little cruel. At least you see now when it started."

She nodded. "I think I saw it all along. I can't imagine why I didn't admit it to myself. When emotions and sex joined hands, that was when the need for something else came to the fore. That and the fact that I could relax and enjoy it so much more when I was a little tight."

"That's all very true. The love couch is not a place for even the slightest inhibition. Enter dignity and complete consciousness, exit ... something. A something that can reduce enjoyment. Tell me, how did you keep out emotional involvement before?"

"There was some involvement, naturally, but nothing that the act didn't satisfy along with the physical. I suppose it was because I was in love with Larsen and never had been before."

He frowned. "Not entirely. There's more to it than that. If you'd been in love with Larsen, you wouldn't have been able to give him up so easily."

Her lovely face seemed to leap at him as she leaned quickly forward. "I became bored with him because I'd taken all he had to give. I drank more and more to try to recapture some of the early ecstasy. Then I got an appetite for drinking. Then came that scene at Westchester and I began to hate myself for doing things no decent woman would do."

"Women who are indecent wouldn't be in your trouble," he assured her. "If you were indecent ... I mean studiedly and deliberately, you wouldn't be upset about it. What was it that really made you take the final step to see me?"

"I thought about suicide, something I *never* did before."

"I see. Well, remember this. You perform badly when you drink, then you drink to force some sort of forgetfulness. It's a circle that could someday drive you to suicide. Don't you think you're worth saving?"

Tears came to her eyes and Dr. Leibermann felt a racketing charge of most unprofessional pity leap through his nerves. She sighed. "I think so. That's the purely selfish outlook. When I think of what I've done, I ask myself why? What makes you important? That's hard to answer."

"This tall lanky Texan...what's his name?"

"Frazer. Craine Frazer. Actually, I think the thought that he had seen me perform was the hardest blow I ever had to take. You see, until these things happened to me in New York, I'd never had to deal with any such emotions. When I was very young and people talked about me, all I did was get belligerent...in mind, at least, and although I resented it, I didn't care enough to let it bother me. When Mrs. Graves caught her son and me in the act, I was actually amused...and she was an amusing sight, believe me. I just didn't care. Now I do. Why?"

"I think you were way ahead of yourself. I mean you were intelligent, precocious probably, but still immature. You didn't realize, really, what the effect of these acts might be. All of a sudden you find someone you want to impress. You could hardly have done a better job in reverse. For the first time you are forced to look at yourself through another's eyes. What you see appalls you and yet you'll go back and get drunk all over again."

She bit her lower lip. "I was a fool not to come to see you earlier. You have no idea how much better I feel. How much more I understand me. You made me talk. You made me admit things...I had to in order to tell you the kind of truth you wanted...admit things I'd never been able to admit to myself. What about the physical addiction?"

Dr. Leibermann placed the tips of his long fingers together. "In your particular case, let me point out a few things. You're not depleted ... not enough for it to show. You have a good solid grasp of the essentials of your trouble. I think you're strong enough to resist the physical craving. With depletion and malnutrition comes a loss of poise, loss of the ability to think coherently, loss of self-respect and loss of every sense of fitness, good taste and social responsibility."

"What about the things I've done?"

"It's true, you've performed rather badly, but you can't say this is from depletion or mental deterioration."

"That seems to make it worse, doesn't it? I have no excuse."

"The search for an excuse has led many into self-illusionment. They think lies so consistently that they can't even be honest with themselves. I have a feeling that in spite of what you've done, the fact that you are revolted by it is a good sign that you're innately decent. When all the bars are down from drinking, you act as any animal would. At the animal level there is no such things as taste and pride. All you have to do is to stay away from that level."

She sighed flutteringly. "When will you start treatment?"

He laughed. "It's already started. From now on, it's up to you. Naturally you won't be able to just shrug the thing off like a dirty shirt. You might get drunk again and act badly. Remember the details of how you fell before and avoid them. Get drunk at home if you have to. Stay away from parties or anything that could develop into drinking. Just remember that when you drink, you act badly and you act badly because you're exposed. Draw yourself a map that will lead to the avoidance of male company when you're drinking. You haven't I don't believe, taken a girlfriend, have you?"

She shrank away from him. "Oh ... *no* ..."

"Then watch it. There are women in New York to whom you'll be just as irresistible as you are to men. With your background so completely devoid of any such thing, you'll hate yourself worse if that ever happens to you. You'll have to examine yourself carefully, admit what you'll do under what provocation and how you will feel about it. Then aim your life to avoid these traps. Some day when maturity has become rooted and solid, maybe you'll be able to drink socially. Maybe you'll be able to step into these traps without getting your legs skinned. That's what I hope to see."

She fumbled with her purse. "I'll pay you now."

"He looked at her keenly. "Do you have a job?"

No."

"Money?"

"I have some saved from my last job."

"Let's sort of wait things out. You might need this money to tide you over to the next job."

Tears came to her eyes again. "You're being very kind, Doctor."

"A psychiatrist who isn't a little more than normally kind should be drowned. I ever saw who could make me sprain my ethics without half trying. You're honest, you're brave, you're strong and just to look at you makes my throat hurt."

She smiled wanly "You're the second man I ever mot who has paid me honest compliments. Frazer was the other. He just mentioned it without emotion, without that sly look, without suggestion. No one who hasn't been along my road knows how warm it feels to be appreciated without the usual idea in the background."

"Yeah," he said with a chuckle, "we're a couple of great guys. Now remember. If you don't see me or call me and let me know how you're doing, I'll be concerned and will probably become unethical by looking you up. I'm interested, a great deal more interested than I ever allow myself to become with a mere patient… mere." Now, we've had a good cathartic session. What say we go home?"

"Fine," she said, getting up.

CHAPTER EIGHT

She decided to walk and have dinner on the way and strangely the sight of brilliantly advertised bars didn't attract her and she became elated. She ate a good dinner notwithstanding the late lunch and dawdled comfortably over her coffee and smoked a cigarette.

The first annoyance came when she reached the apartment. The phone was ringing. Her heart leaped at the thought that it just might be Craine Frazer but she knew he didn't know where she lived. Larsen and Colton had found her. He could find her if he wanted to badly enough.

It was Colton weeping and begging again. A titanic fury erupted in her and she slammed the instrument down hard enough to shatter it. She turned, still strumming with rage and took a drink from a bottle straight before she realized what she had done.

She crumpled at the knees and sank to the floor, her hands tight against her temples. "What'll I do?"

The first thing she did after recovering from the shock of her subconscious act was to repeat it consciously until she was in a delightful haze. Providentially, she fell asleep and her couch was soft enough that she slept all night and woke the next morning refreshed with no hangover. She felt encouraged and at least there wasn't the knowledge that she had bellied around in the gutter. Infection ... She shrank from the word and prayed that the penicillin worked. She almost made herself sick thinking about it and more to have something to do than anything else, she sat down and packaged three stories that she chose at random and mailed them to the best weekly magazine in the country. Crowders Magazine was the big weekly slick that budding authors always think of publishing in and many send their first efforts with high hopes, a vast percentage of which are dashed with the cryptic rejection, "Sorry but this is not for us." mailed them. She window-shopped and resolutely refused to even look toward a bar. She ate a good dinner that evening and went home in bed dead tired.

Craine Frazer sat in his office and admired the rich paneling and the impeccable appointments. He had been in this office for a year when by virtue of his father's stock in Crowder Publishing Company, he could have almost written his own ticket. To the surprise of many he had caught on soundly and in the editorial office was held in deep respect. He had made a number of radical decisions since he had been in his editorial chair and they paid off handsomely. The last decision on whether or not a story should be published rested with him and in any number of cases he had come into violent disagreement with some of his staff readers as to what constituted the proper material.

"This is a family magazine," he had said. "We'll leave the rarified literary gems for the *Yale Review* and such. The people who read our magazine want to be amused, instructed or entertained. We'll vary it up and down the scale so no one can say, as they have in the past. with some justification, 'Read one Crowder story and you've read them all'."

He made his decisions stick and Crowders, always prosperous, became more so and circulation the pulse beat of any publication soared. If circulation is the pulse beat, advertising is the life blood and any office boy knows the importance of the former to the latter.

As one of the editors of Crowders, it fell to Frazer to see agents and his feeling for the breed was mixed. Some were stalwarts in the field of marketing. They rarely brought him a manuscript that was incorrectly slanted or too far afield for Crowders editorial policies. Some were importunate salesmen who tried to unload sub-standard material by sales pitch. Those he soon identified and for them it was virtually impossible to get an appointment. There was one rather special agent for whom he had achieved almost affection. Bern Wolff could saunter into Frazer's office and take a drink from the office bottle any time he chose. They had met at breakfast that morning to discuss a serial Wolff was trying to place. Frazer rarely ate breakfast outside his own apartment simply because few if any restaurants in New York could boast of a chef who could rival the priceless Amanda who had been his watchdog since she was twelve and he a squalling infant.

So as Wolff ate a sparing breakfast, Frazer sipped at a cup of coffee. "I wouldn't bring this to you, Craine," Wolff said, "if I didn't think it had something. It'll have to be shortened about eight thousand words but the kid'll eat up the chance. He's got something I think you could use."

"Well, what's your problem?"

"I don't want this thing turned down so far below you that you'll never hear a thin faint cry. I want you to read it. You know I don't come to your place loaded with duds. If the flics don't grab this up, I don't know Hollywood. Also I know Max Manns well enough to know it won't hardback unless you publish it and I already have Knudson's promise to do the full length in the hardback if you'll serialize it first."

Frazer lit one of his long cigarettes. "All right, Bern, I'll look at it. My reading staff thinks I'm a sort of peculiar, anyway, so their feelings are already hurt."

Wolff lifted his lined saturnine face and grimaced. "Your readers...don't give me your readers. I know this much. The circulation department and advertising think you're a little tin god. You didn't get that way by being peculiar. One of these days, I've always been promising myself, this racket is going to come up with someone without delusions of a literary Julius Caesar and really tune in on what the public wants to read and give it to them. You're pretty close to being elected."

Frazer's face was sober. "Thanks. For your part, you don't bring me stuff that'd fit some pulp tabloid type of thing and waste my peoples' time rejecting it."

"By the way, how's Elaine doing with the slush pile?"

"Great. She's come up with six acceptable stories in the last year. I don't think the pile averaged one a year before her. She showed me two that she wanted to get the authors to work on further. She did and they did and we had to reject them anyhow."

"Why? Bad jobs?"

No. The jobs were perfect and we could have used them, but did you ever stop to think how many good stories must be rejected, stories that we could use easily but can't because we're loaded?"

"I guess you must really have some poundage come in, I'm a sucker for young writers myself and my turnover is fearful. I can't shove them off as easy as you either."

"Last year," said Frazer dragging deeply on his cigarette, 'we had a total of two hundred and eighty-two thousand manuscripts submitted.

Wolff sighed. "I'm a writer myself, you know … nonfiction. I had a couple published that sold several million copies. But I was a newcomer and got taken on the contracts. I have a feeling for writers. I know what goes on in their minds.

"Well, I'll look at your boy's stuff. Send it attention my office so it won't have to go through the mill. Come on up and have a breakfast snort."

"Sure will. Your liquor, from the delight of it, must have come over with Columbus."

As they walked down Lexington toward the Palace. Frazer examined his agent friend as he had done many times in the past. He was small, maybe five-four with big bony shoulders. His clothes never seemed to fit and he had the habit of balling his fists up and ramming them into his jacket pockets.

They turned into the Palace at Lexington and were whisked upward to the sprawling empire of Crowders that occupied acres. There seemed to be a constant bustle of people going and coming through the offices and corridors and one of them a girl, coming out of a door with a tremendous load of material, bumped into Frazer and lost half her load.

The girl reeled against the wall, recovered and gasped an apology, her load … manuscripts in manila envelopes scattered all across the corridor.

Wolff smiled lightly. "Ah … the lovely Elaine Ward, Empress of the slush pile.

"I had … them stacked … so high …" She bent over to pick them up. "… that I couldn't see. I'm awful sorry."

They helped her pick up her load and as further assistance carried them to her office.

Wolff chuckled as he put his pile on the desk. "Marvelle Martingale … what a name. It does look like if people have to have a pen name, they wouldn't be so damned alliterative."

"*What'd you say?*" Frazer whirled like a flash, his usually tame eyes burning.

"Well … hell, I just said …"

"Here, let me see that." Frazer almost pushed the smaller man aside reaching for the top envelope. He snatched it up and looked at it hard. "Marvelle Martingale, all right, and you're wrong, Bern, that's really her name."

"How do you know?"

"I know her," he said shortly. "Miss Ward, I want … no, I'll take it with me, This I must see and firsthand."

As they walked toward Frazer's office, Wolff said, "Boy, for a moment I thought you were coming undone. This gal must be something."

Frazer didn't say anything as he opened his door and tossed the envelope into a wire basket on his desk, "She's something all right. The bottle's in the usual place."

Wolff laughed and held the bottle up to the light. "There's enough for two. I know you're not a morning drinker, but today you might break the rule. You were pretty pale in Elaine's office."

"Knock it off," said Frazer, "and make me one, too."

They took seats and sipped their drinks, Wolff watching Frazer intently. "I'm a supersensitive sort, as you well know. Perceptive and all that. How come that name upset you so?"

"It's a long story."

"Not the way you tell it. You going to read her stuff?"

"Yes ... when you leave."

"I demand you read it now."

"Why?"

"Because I want to watch your face when you see this lovely creature come up with a dud."

Frazer lit one of his cigarry cigarettes. "Bern, stop heckling me. I know the kid . . hell, that's all she is. She's loaded to the scuppers with more pure damn animal magnetism than I ever saw in all the women in my life put together ... and she's an alcoholic. When she alcoholizes, she becomes fundamental ... has no restraint whatever."

"Then you must have had a ball."

"I did not. I didn't touch her."

"Then everything you know is hearsay, not knowledge."

"I saw."

"Oh ..." Wolff lifted his dark eyes. "Want to tell me?"

"Someday maybe. Not now. After all, it's not just my secret."

The agent nodded. "Sure. I can piece it in, I guess, You had her picked for something better than that."

"Correct. Now I got work to do. Bring me your boy's stuff. I'll see that it gets a fair shake."

"Okay. I enjoyed the drink and the sight of you bucked out of that Texas calm."

"Get out."

"Sure ... sure, but I'll be back."

Frazer leaned back, studied the calendar his secretary had aligned for the day. He leaned forward and punched the button on his intercom. "Miss Allen, please come in for a moment."

Miss Allen walked into the office. "Did I load your day too much?"

"Oh no." He didn't look up because she disturbed him vaguely.

"This man from King Books," he said, "he can have *Ankle Deep in Clover* with the usual reprint contract. It won't be picked up for the hardback by Harris House like we first thought and this man from Clarkson ... I don't want to see him because he thinks he's doing us and Carl Strom a favor by publishing a collection of Strom's shorts. You can mail out the regular routine check on that."

"But you said we were overloaded on that kind, too," she reminded him.

"I've decided we'll load up a little heavier on that type of story. They go very well and they're just controversial enough to get a good load of reader mail."

"Was that Wolff that came in with you?"

"Yes ... why?"

"I don't like him."

He looked up and smiled. "Don't bother. I can't think of a man who'd care less."

"Elaine left another of her duds on your desk."

"Elaine has come up with more publishable 'duds' from the slush pile than anyone we ever had in there."

"I know but to me a slush pile is well-named."

"That's probably why you're a secretary, Miss Allen. That's all for now."

She turned on her heel and switched out disapprovingly. He picked up the manila envelope with Marvelle Martingale's name and return address and stared at it for some time. He opened it, took out the contents, and stopped short. He wanted an unbiased opinion on it before he looked at a word. He could tell that they were not long … maybe thirty-five hundred to four thousand words. He flicked a key on his intercom. "Miss Murdock, are you busy?"

"No, Mr. Frazer. Can I do something for you?"

"Could you come to my office for ten minutes?"

"I think so. Mr. Crowder hasn't come in yet."

Mr. Crowder was, nominally at least president of Crowder Publications. In fact, he was a little more than a figurehead and held his job because of a block of stock and his name. He was sensible enough to occupy his office, draw his salary and leave the running of the business to smarter men, such as Craine Frazer. Miss Murdock, his secretary, was the oldest working employee and as smart as a whip. She was sixty years old, acerbic, outspoken and worth her salary to keep Crowder happy with his crown.

She came in, spare, sharp-faced with hawkish amber eyes. "Well, Longhorn, what has you stumped this morning?"

"Sit down, Gert, and don't badger me. Wolff just left and I'm still sore from his biting."

She sniffed disdainfully. "I'd send that whiskey-swilling ten-percenter packing."

"I have a manuscript here that I'm afraid to read."

"Whatever for?"

"Well … it happens that I know the girl who wrote it. I think you'll understand me when I say I don't think I could take an unbiased attitude. Read it. If it stinks, tell me and I won't even glance at it."

"Ummm … she's that cute, hunh?"

"Cute is hardly the word for her, but go ahead and see what you think. I haven't forgotten that you were some big help here when I was trying to change policy around a little."

"It was more than a little and the business can thank us ... You for having the savvy and me for being dumb enough to love you and therefore support you. Gimme the stuff."

She read while he relaxed in his chair, feet on desk, his cordovan boots glimmering richly, and smoked a cigarette. When at last he looked at her she was seated stiffly looking at him, her eyes swimming in tears.

"I could bash your head in, Longhorn. I don't go for your type of joke."

"I beg your pardon."

"Don't get devious. You read this! You knew what you had but you dragged me in here ... Come to think of it, just why did you drag me in here?"

"To begin with, I didn't drag you. You walked in. I'd never seen the stuff before. I haven't read it. I was afraid to for the reason I gave you. Why all the tears?"

Miss Murdock tapped the manuscript with stiff fingers. "Longhorn, this is the most exquisitely sensitive thing I ever read in my life. It fairly tears your heart out and it's not one of the usual tear-jerkers at all. No death scenes. It's a soul hung out to dry with every cranny and wrinkle for the eye to see. Remember Hubert Waxley?"

"Yes. He died last year."

"Correct. Hubert Waxley was the only man I ever knew whose mind was orderly enough to just melt a story and your it on paper. She's like him, maybe more so. It reminds me of a situation ... This sounds silly but there's story that's got to come out.

Although he laughed, Frazer felt a chill at his spine. Gaffer would do anything, including handing out spy money, to get a good writer. Frazer knew if Gaffer saw this story or anyone on his staff with half a mind, Cosmos would buy it instantly. It was good if it could wring tears from an old trooper like Miss Murdock and stimulate her into an analysis of the writer.

"All right, Gert, what would you do?"

"I'd get her down here so fast her head would swim, get her on an exclusive contract as tight as the bung in a barrel. When you read it, think what a really good director could do with it. If a producer could coax half the simplicity and sensitivity from this story to a celluloid he'd be an academy award winner. I know you think I've flipped my lid ... you just read it and tell me."

Instead of reading it, Frazer went to war with himself and just before he went home that afternoon he had another visit from Miss Murdock.

"Read that story?" she barked.

"Er ... well, I didn't. I was pretty busy ..."

"You're a twenty-two carat liar. Give me the other two. I want to read them tonight."

His face was tinged with pink as he handed her the other manuscripts.

CHAPTER NINE

Miss Murdock ate a quick meal at Toffinetti's before going to her apartment. She kicked off her shoes, lit a cigarette and proceeded to make herself comfortable. She felt a subdued excitement that she rarely felt toward reading material. The first of Marvelle's stories she read had tugged at her heartstrings in a manner she had not experienced in thirty years, and she was anxious to see if the girl was good or once-lucky.

She read slowly and soon discovered that no luck was involved with this kind of writing. The girl had a style as fresh as a breath of cool spring air and as she had seen in the first one, words flowed with an ease, fitness and grace she had never seen equaled before. Her joys were multicolored, her contentments almost soporific, her loves tender and happy, her sadnesses and griefs almost unbearable.

"This," she said aloud, sitting bolt upright and tense, "is uncanny."

She sat back but soon she was tensed and sitting on the edge of her chair again. She picked the phone from an end table and dialed.

"Amanda, is that snake-gutted employer of yours there yet? Good, put him on." She lit another cigarette. "Longhorn, have you had dinner? Good. I want you to go somewhere with me on company business."

The phone squawked resentfully, but she shook her head. "No, it can't wait until tomorrow. I won't sleep a wink unless we get it done tonight...No, I can't tell you what it's about. I'll take a cab and pick you up in fifteen minutes." She hung up on his protests, slipped into her coat, grabbed her purse and left the apartment.

"Where are we going?" he asked grumpily as he get into the cab.

"To see that girl. I read those other two. Longhorn, we've *got* to get her under contract."

"Tonight?"

"Well, I'd do it tonight but we'd have to go by the office and get a form. I want a verbal commitment."

"I wish to hell you hadn't dragged me along," he said in a half mutter.

"I gather that, but why?"

He frowned. "Gert, will you give me your word never to reveal a word of this if I tell you?"

"Cross my creaking old heart. Is it bad?"

"Terrible."

"Good. I haven't been properly shocked since Crowder broke his glasses and pinched my behind thinking it was Valerie."

He told her, digging deep into his store of euphemisms so the shock wouldn't be too great. When he finished she was crying.

"Now what?" he asked, startled.

"Shut up and let me think." It didn't take long. "I don't know what to think, but I'll tell you one thing for sure. I believe every word you say and yet I have a certain concrete knowledge that she isn't what all this would seem to make her."

"What makes you say that?"

"Because I am as certain as it is humanly possible to be that this girl could *not* be what the evidence supports and write the way she does. I'm not a fool, you know, and my favorite reading is psychiatry. Something ... maybe her drinking, cuts her off completely from reality ... her kind of reality. She is, in fact, two people. Now I can see some things I missed before you told me the story. She has more than the normal appreciation for dignity and good taste. A hack could be an atheist and write for a church journal. Not this kid. This stuff she writes comes from deep inside her and I don't give a tinker's dam *what* the evidence says."

He sat back and heaved a seismic sigh. "Now I'm glad I came."

"Why?"

"Because now I know why I've had a war going on inside me since I went to that party. Funny how I could feel something and not be able to identify it and you reveal the depth of it by a logical conscious process."

"Well, I'm smarter'n you are, for one thing. For another, you're too young to know how to get on speaking terms with your subconscious. Some would say you instinctively had trouble believing what your eyes told you. I say the evidence was there and your other mind couldn't accept what your consciousness was asking. Therefore, the war."

"You're the greatest, Gert," he said with a sigh. "Now I'm in a devil of a fix for sure."

"Why?"

"Because as long as I could half believe she was bad, I had no emotional involvement. You've obliterated that end of it pretty well, but not well enough. I suppose I'm Victorian enough to let it set up a canker in my mind."

"So you're emotionally involved now. Pretty quick work, wouldn't you say?"

"Yes. You've just read her stuff. Wait till you see her."

Miss Murdock crossed her thin legs. "Well, Buster, you'd better get hold of yourself. The chances are she wouldn't give you a damp cracker."

"Yes," he said softly. "That's a point to think about."

She put a wrinkled hand on his. "Look, Longhorn, you're my boy. If she's half as smart as we think she is, she won't be able to resist you, but there's one thing. Don't you hurt that kid. You get all that poison out of you mind before you get her involved. Hear me, boy?"

"Yes, ma'am. I hear you..."

The cab had pulled to the curb and the driver was holding the door open for them.

They found the apartment and Frazer wished again that he hadn't come, but his reasons were different. He didn't examine the matter too closely but now he was frankly afraid. Of what he couldn't say.

Miss Murdock pressed the buzzer and though they waited a long time, got no answer. She rang again, insistently, but still no answer.

"Maybe she's out," said Frazer, hoping that she was.

"Maybe, but after coming this far, I'm going to make sure." So she went to her knees and peered beneath the door. "That light's on," she muttered half to herself. She got up and tried the door. It was not locked, so they walked in.

That morning Marvelle had awakened so depressed that she cried as she tried to eat a little breakfast. Through her mind all the good things that had ever happened to her paraded tantalizingly. She remembered the irretrievable nights warm and content in Cannonball Barton's arms. She relived the caress of his hands on her silken thighs, the touch of his lips on her high pink-tipped breasts. She remembered nights with Colton, nights with Larsen when he would so lose himself in the breathless wonder of her love that he'd go quietly mad and play her as though she were a magnificent musical instrument.

She dressed and went down the street with the idea of looking for a job. She still had some money but she owed the psychiatrist... she had not the faintest notion how much, and she knew her little nest egg was being fast depleted. She never allowed the thought to make a real appearance but she knew that the taste for liquor was one reason why it was dropping so alarmingly.

She was so despondent that she passed up several possibilities she had located in the classified ads but finally she went into an office that had advertised for fresh faces for television. The ad was vague and left a great deal unsaid.

The offices of the firm were beautifully decorated with rich deep carpets and expensive furniture. The president, whom she finally saw, was encased in an office that might have come from some modem "Arabian Nights." The president, a Mr. Neverson, was big, expensively barbered and tailored with searching brown eyes and thick curly brown hair.

"Miss Martingale, is it?" She nodded and felt his eyes searching her body like probing fingers.

"Yes," she said. His gaze excited her but his person repelled her.

"I'm Frank Neverson," he said effusively. "Please be seated."

She sat and crossed her legs and as she expected, his eyes followed the movement with care.

"Now, Miss Martingale, I take it you wish to matriculate in our school?"

She looked at him blankly. "School?"

"Why yes ... er, what was it you had in mind?"

"I'm looking for a job. Your ad didn't say anything about a school. You said 'Television is looking for new faces. Let us fix yours'."

He nodded. "Of course. Television can always use new faces. That's our business. We train you, teach you how to walk, to act, voice culture, everything that any aspiring girl would have to know in order to break in. A gratifying number of our students have made the grade." He waved his hand to a wall that was nearly covered with pictures, some of whom she recognized as bit players. There were star's pictures, too, but from where she sat she couldn't see that they were just autographed pictures that could be bought in hundreds of places in New York or free if one would write for them.

She shook her head. "I don't care about schooling. I am looking for a job."

He shook his head chidingly. "You can't do it, Miss Martingale."

"Do what?"

"You can't keep such beauty from the public. It isn't fair. It isn't sporting. You were born to be admired..." He laughed liquidly. "To be loved, to enthrall audiences. You belong to the world, Miss Martingale. It is unthinkable that you should keep yourself hidden from the thirsting public." He leaned forward suddenly. "Please, don't say anything. Let me make you a proposition. Suppose we submit to you a potential estimate and let's see what will come from it. It will cost you nothing. Then if you still don't wish to enroll...." He shrugged and spread his hands.

"What is a potential estimate?"

He opened a drawer and took out an impressive sheet. "This is it. It takes in everything you have. General appearance...and believe me, Miss Martingale, that is something. Figure..." He sighed suggestively. "Legs, hips, waist and bust...the works."

Marvelle was intrigued. If this was a pitch, and she half suspected that it was, the man certainly had a readymade beginning.

She smiled. "All right. What have I got to lose?"

He bustled around making considerable to-do with preparation. He turned to her with tape in hand. "Now, Miss Martingale, this is usually the hard part for most beautiful women. So few of them, not already professionals, care to disrobe before me."

"Professional what?" she asked blandly.

"Professional..." He stopped and gulped, then recovered, but not before blood had dyed his face. He chuckled embarrassedly. "You're a wit, Miss Martingale, but if you'd like to get along with it..."

She directed her effective eyes straight at him. "You mean with the disrobing?"

"Yes. You see, there are many things I have to know. There is no such thing as a perfectly symmetrical figure. This chart, a copy of which you'll have to take with you to interviews, is of great value in making up costumes, wardrobes and the like, in order to make the utmost of what you have. It is quite obvious that you have a great deal and we certainly want to make the most of it."

She shrugged. "Very well. Will you move that other chair over here so I can drape my clothes on it?"

"Of course... of course. Most of them prefer a screen but since I always require that they step out for my examination it seems a little silly."

"Yes, doesn't it? I won't need the screen."

Marvelle hated herself for what she was about to do, but not enough to change her mind. So the old lecher wanted a free show? Well, she'd give him one, but if he thought he was going to stretch her on the casting couch, he had another think coming.

She sat on one chair and placed her coat on the other. Carefully and with deliberation she drew up a leg until she could reach a shoe, the effect was so upsetting to Mr. Neverson that he almost gave vocal evidence of it, catching himself just in time. She faced him and the length of shimmering leg with its lacquered coating of nylon was enough to make his eyes bulge. Above the stocking tops was an expanse of the finest thigh he had ever seen, strong, rounded and clothed in the most mouth-watering skin he could imagine... all the way to where the thin tricot of her briefs clung to her legs and middle. He swallowed jerkily as she drew up the other leg and removed the shoe and stocking... slowly, tantalizingly. The effect was even better because she hadn't pulled down her skirt that had been hoist when she pulled the first leg up. Her skin shone like mellow ivory through the sheerness of her briefs. Mr. Neverson, long a connoisseur of the form divine, was in a nest of ants but not once had she raised her eyes to examine his reaction. For this he was subconsciously grateful. He was a little frightened because his usual reaction upon seeing a revealed woman was one of enjoyment which usually caused him to plot and plan and his percentage of reward was high. This was something else entirely. It was like seeing a woman disrobe for the first time.

When she had removed her stockings and shoes, she stood up. She had worn a simple skirt of heavy black silk and an equally simple turquoise sweater. She unbuttoned the sweater, slipped it off, leaving only her bra, filled to the brim with succulent flesh, firm, upstanding, magnificent. She stood bolt upright, making the most of her upshot breasts, undid one button of the skirt waistband, unzipped it and let it slide downward. Deftly she caught it before it reached the floor, bending deep and letting him get a long look at the pure sculpture of her back and the fecund curve of her hips. She tossed the skirt to the chair and reaching back undid the bra catch. It followed the skirt to the chair. Mr. Neversen made a strangling sound deep in his throat. Every move she had made since she started undressing excited her more and more until by the time she slid her briefs from her waist and tossed them on the chair, she was in a ferment. Her body was feverish with demand when at last she looked up, and stretching one arm high, placed the other hand on her hip and made a slow graceful turn... then she looked at him. She had been fairly certain that he was merely a middle-aged lecher who drooled at the sight of lovely women. He'd probably make suggestive but oblique advances, possibly try to put his hands on her. He could hardly afford to attempt rape in his office.

The instant she saw his face, she knew she had been all wrong. His face was frozen in a look of such shock that she gasped and her already racing blood speeded up. She knew that she had presented him with something new in bodies, something that for all his experience, he had not been prepared for. He gasped, licked his lips and his hands clenched and unclenched spasmodically. His eyes were glazed and he started toward her and it was then that she realized that this was another time when she had misjudged her own powers of resistance, that her earlier resolution had been a mistake, that her bones were water, her muscles milk, her voice stuck in her throat. When his arms encircled her, she felt relieved and her mind swirled in an insane vortex and begged him on. The shiny leather of the couch was a chill to her skin that scarcely registered and victory brought a musical note from so deep within her that it seemed not even of female voice but the subdued throaty announcement of nature that another battle had been won. Later, she lay in the calm backwaters sobbing with relief. He hardly existed as a man at all but someone... a very vague someone of the male of the species who had brought her a much needed release from the savage demand that had so sorely rent her.

By gradual degrees she returned to reality. The wool of his worsted suit prickled her skin and his hot gushing breath fanned her neck and shoulders. He became a man... then a man whom she had resolved to turn around and deny what he wanted most... then Mr. Neversen whom she'd shocked so badly that he slipped back to his youth and was drawn into the quicksands of her attraction without being able to stop, without being able to utter a word.

Suddenly she hated herself with a passion that struck her like a charge of hot dirty water. She made a vicious twisting lunge that as heavy as he was sent him falling backward to sprawl on the floor, ludicrous, astonished but still speechless. She leaped to her feet and started dressing. She was dressed and putting on her coat when he came up from the floor. He had found his voice and words poured from him in a beseeching torrent.

"I don't know what happened to me, Miss... er, Miss Martingale. It never happened before, believe me. You wanted a job. I'll arrange one. It doesn't matter what you can do and just for the advertising we'll underwrite any instruction you'd wish to take. Please... a job, free tutelage." He was sweating and frantic. "I apologize from the bottom of my heart. Really I do... a job... anything you wish... instructions..."

She walked out, leaving him babbling offers as fast as he could think them up.

She turned in at the very first bar she could find and ordered a triple bourbon. She had finished it and was feeling the hot soaring beat of it through her blood when she remembered that Dr. Liebermann had told her never to get drunk in public. With a sob she turned and almost ran out.

She hailed a cab and by the time she reached her apartment she was crying hard and wanting a drink so badly that she would have given her last cent for one. She took one straight as soon as she could open a bottle, then she stripped and running the tub full of water scoured herself viciously as though wanting to remove even the skin wherever he had touched. All through the bath and the subsequent harsh rubdown with a rough towel, she cried steadily and silently.

She took another drink, then another, sprawled nakedly on the couch with the bottle nearby on the coffee table. She closed her mind and in order to keep it closed and as far from the horror of the morning as possible, she kept drinking. Outlines in the room grew fuzzy and her thinking chaotic. She thought of suicide again and her body was rent by a convulsion of denial. She buried her face in a pillow and screamed until she was breathless and sweating. Time meant nothing now and her movements grew palsied as she handled the bottle until at last it slipped from her nerveless fingers and rolled on the floor, gurgling out the last of its contents.

She sat up with great effort, weaving, fearfully drunk, trying to focus her eyes but unable to locate the bottle. With a moan of desperate anguish, she slipped back to the prone position. She hiccoughed a few times and a violent shudder rippled her musculature ... then she passed out.

When they saw her on the couch, she had twisted but not completed the turn and was so gracefully distorted that Frazer caught his breath. She was perfectly nude and even in the slack-mouthed sleep of the very drunk, her loveliness throttled Miss Murdock, the spinster, as well as Frazer, the young male.

He caught his breath in such a searing gasp that Miss Murdock cast him an annoyed glance. She turned back and looked at the girl again. She cleared her throat. "I suppose I should say something, but for the life of me I don't know what it should be. I'm talking now because I'm afraid not to … not that I'm saying anything."

"Poor kid," he said so softly that she shot him a questioning glance.

"Why 'poor kid'?"

"She's in the grip of an addiction, she's all alone in the big city. She's small town … out of her element. She has depth, exquisite sensitivity and yet she's not hypersensitive. I hope you follow me."

"I'm way ahead of you, Longhorn. I've read her stuff. You haven't. She's the type who, if she had to keep herself out of her material, couldn't write."

He fidgeted and' tried to swallow the lump in his throat. "Shouldn't we cover her or something?"

"In good time. Right now I'm enjoying hating myself when I was her age. For years I've remembered myself as a particularly succulent chick, stroking my ego in assuming under my breath, so to speak, that the best man in the world was about one quarter good enough for me. I was never at my glowingest within yelling distance of this child. I was probably about one third what I thought I was." She rubbed her eyes. "When you read her writing, there will be another thing that'll strike you. One already has."

"What's that?"

"Her as a person and her writing. They're both just a shade improbable." She sighed and shook her head. "All right. You may cover her now. I've hated myself enough for one evening. By the way, you won't leave her here like this, will you?"

"Why not?"

She uttered an enraged snort. "Oh … dammit, Longhorn, I could slap you. Unlocked door, as toothsome a dainty as any rapist could dream up…Have you lost your mind? And you think she's drunk. Do you know it? How do you know she didn't drink whiskey to get up the nerve to swallow a handful of sleeping pills?"

Frazer came alive with such speed that he went a little dizzy. "What'll we do? Take her to the hospital?"

"Wait a moment." She sat beside the girl and felt her pulse and watched her respiration. "Pulse about normal for a drunk. She's breathing good. Tell you what. Let's get something on her and take her to my apartment. An impressionable young doctor who has just gone into practice has an adjoining apartment. She'll upset him so, he'll stay with her half the night if need be."

"That sounds all right to me."

Dr. John Hands was young and impressionable as Miss Murdock had said. He proved no more proof against Marvelle's now helpless beauty than other men had, and his examination was painstaking. He finally sat up and faced them. "In most cases of barbiturate poisoning, which is far and away the favorite for sleeping pills, there is general depression of respiration and heart action. I find no such depression."

"What was all that about?" asked Miss Murdock.

"To test her reflexes. They are considerably lowered in response but that might easily be from the alcohol she has consumed. Her pupils are within normal limits. They react to light."

"Wouldn't an overdose of whiskey do pretty much the same thing as sleeping pills?" asked Miss Murdock.

"The picture," said the young doctor seriously, "while similar in many details, is not a duplication. Actually, she doesn't appear to have had a great deal of alcohol. By that I mean for the normal person. Notice there is no stertorous breathing. Her respiration is slower and deeper and there is some cardiac depression, but her pulse rate is sixty-five and that is not too low. Her pupils are not dilated, which you would expect in a case of deep alcoholic narcosis. Her color is good and she doesn't appear to be *in extremis.* Now several things suggest themselves. Either she is not accustomed to alcohol and reacted quickly to a relatively small amount...this is unlikely because amount is a personal relative thing. For instance three drinks might, in me, take on the symptomatic manifestation of ten in you. Or she drank under great emotional tension. That would make some difference. Just what I'm not prepared, fully, to say The most likely choice is that she was terribly fatigued either emotionally, physically or both, drank a good amount of whiskey, then fell into an exhausted sleep which was deepened by the narcotic effect of alcohol until it was almost a state of anesthesia. Maybe also she is now on the tail end of a jag. In which case, the earlier and more pronounced symptoms might have disappeared. I think I can safely say that she has no barbiturate poisoning. Would either of you know whether she has suicidal tendencies?"

"I'd say not," replied Frazer. "She has had some acute emotional problems lately and they might contribute to the seeking of oblivion...the alcohol, I mean, but I've noticed no suicidal tendencies. However, neither of us knows her that well. I'm merely offering an unsupported opinion."

The doctor got up. "I think she should be watched for an hour or so just to see if any further symptoms arise." He turned to Miss Murdock. "I'll be up for an hour or so working on a paper. If you wish, I'll drop in before I go to bed."

"That'd be fine, Doctor," she said. "I'll have some coffee, tea or chocolate ready for you."

He grinned personally. "I'm a coffee hog and it never keeps me awake. I'll come in just before I go to bed."

He left and Frazer emitted a tremendous "whoof" that startled Miss Murdock and she looked around for something to throw.

"Well, I'm glad that's settled," he said with relief.

"You needn't blow me out of my skin because of it," she snapped. "Will you have coffee?"

"I'd love some. Can I help make it?"

"No. You stay there and watch sleeping beauty for symptoms."

"I'm afraid I wouldn't recognize one while looking at her."

"How do you mean?"

"I mean your amorous intentions. I wasn't kidding when I told you I didn't want you toying with her or subjecting her to any effects of Victorian emotional indigestion."

He shrugged and grinned ruefully. "Gert, I can't answer questions like that. I'll certainly not hurt her knowingly."

"You'd better not," she said ominously as she disappeared into the kitchen.

Dr. Hand came in nearly two hours later, pronounced her improved and in no danger, drank his coffee and departed.

"I didn't know you were so loaded with the milk of human kindness," said Frazer.

"There are any number of things you don't know," she retorted. "However, I must say that I was on this child's side before I met her. Ordinarily I think authors become in a story what they'd like to be in reality. She is different to the extent that I don't believe she portrays any wish fancy."

He smiled. "You're someone who reads psychology and there you are slipping into instinct."

She glared at him then smiled. "Oh … I guess so. It's awfully hard to be scientific when someone like her is involved.

"Speaking of doctors, don't you think she's ripe for a psychiatrist?"

"Of the right sort … yes. Of the other sort, no. By the way. I did some digging in her purse and I came on a card, Aaron Leibermann, M.D. I had a friend who went to him. She thought he was just about the finest because he spent a great deal of his time bearing down on the importance of her mind … singular. That it was a good mind and it was the thing that would cure her, if anything would. That he'd curry it, move it about, wash it out and cause a general upheaval, but in the end her own mental stamina would be the big thing."

"How right was he?"

"With anyone who isn't hopeless, he was a hundred percent right. The other school makes the patient feel that 'Here is a good stout arm to hang on to' and they polish that attitude to such an extent at fifty dollars an hour that the patient becomes addicted to this support. Some even have the money to take their crutch everywhere they go and are afraid to move without his presence or his advice. I want no part of that sort of thing, either for me or anyone I'm interested in."

"Do you suppose she's been to him?"

"I'll find out all about it tomorrow. Now you blow. I need some sleep."

CHAPTER TEN

arvelle woke to strange surroundings again and her first impulse was to leap from the bed and race madly to some sticky doom provided by the first open window. For a long time she lay still looking at the ceiling in the dim light of early morning. She had slept a long time and physically she was refreshed with only the stagnation in her mouth, a slight ringing of her ears and a fullness of her head to tattle on the previous day's libations.

With compressed lips, she fought her emotions, her chin trembling like a hurt child's. Tears flooded her eyes and drew trails of crystal from the outer corners toward her ears. Morning came slowly turning the apartment from grey to its natural colors with soft-footed deliberation. The world outside turned from dusky purple to pink, then the sun peeped up out of the Atlantic.

Miss Murdock awoke and sat up on the sofa, swiveled her head and met the startled eyes of the girl. "Ah ... we're awake."

Marvelle didn't speak but watched the older woman, thoughts tearing through her head. Was this woman one of those the psychiatrist had mentioned ... a female who found her as attractive as had men?

Miss Murdock, in order to evade the enormous searching violet eyes, bustled about donning her robe and snatching the cover from the couch. She returned the couch to sitting attitude, stacked the covers and without another glance at the bed went into the tiny kitchen and started coffee.

Marvelle clung to her equilibrium figuratively with both hands. She couldn't recall leaving the apartment but she obviously had. Had she gone to a bar? Had this woman picked her up before a man had the opportunity? A wave of furious disgust and nausea slammed her so hard that she grew dizzy and almost blacked out.

Miss Murdock came in soon carrying a cup of strong fragrant coffee. "Now my dear. Suppose we start with a cup of good coffee, then we'll talk. All right?"

Marvelle sat up slowly. She wore a nightgown of Miss Murdock's and it far too tight in places. "Please... before anything... How did I get here?"

"We brought you here. A friend of mine and I... We went to your apartment to speak to you about some business. This man friend was along. You were somewhat the worse for wear, so rather than leave you alone, we brought you to my place. Now drink your coffee, then we'll talk."

Meekly Marvelle accepted the coffee and drank it, enjoying the stimulating effect of the hot liquid on her stomach. Her relief at finding that she hadn't been picked up by either man or woman was such that her eyes dripped tears all the while she sipped the hot brew. Miss Murdock watched her and felt like crying too. No one had any right to such loveliness... she squelched the ignoble thought. She was strangely attracted to this child... she seemed a child to Miss Murdock. What were the tears for? What had happened to make an alcoholic out of her?

Marvelle sighed and handed the cup back. "I can't imagine what business you'd have to talk over with me. I have been in New York a year but in that time ..." She shrugged. "I just can't imagine."

"Didn't you submit some manuscripts to Crowder's?"

Marvelle managed a wry chuckle. "Oh... yes, I did. I was bored stiff and had to keep busy to keep from going mad. I write all the time... a release, sort of. I have stacks and stacks of rough drafts. I mailed the manuscripts all right but..." Her eyes shot up and met Miss Murdock's. "It isn't about those awful things, is it?"

Miss Murdock laughed. "I heard a writer say once that he was his own worst critic. I think I know now what he meant. Now I want you to brace yourself. I've been with Crowder's since I was twenty. In that time I've read many a good story and a couple of million that stank to heaven. Not since I drew my first paycheck have I seen a story that could match those you submitted."

Marvelle blinked. "Are you sure I'm awake?"

"I feel safe in saying you are."

The girl shook her head hard and blinked again. "What was the business about. I mean ... what ...?"

"Oh ... the business. Well, it was about the manuscripts, naturally. I could be shot for a traitor but I'm going to tell you a few things you should know. First, although it's not official yet, I feel safe in telling you that they will be accepted, all three of them. You'll be totally out of your element when you visit our offices. Unless I'm mistaken, you know nothing about the business side of publishing and writing."

"I know nothing," said Marvelle profoundly. "Absolutely nothing."

"So I thought. So, first I want you to come with an agent when you come. Crowder's will want an exclusive contract. Sometimes that's good and sometimes not. You need a good agent to advise you."

"But I know no agents."

"That's a small matter. I'll get you one."

Marvelle smiled. "You know, you've done me a few great favors and I don't even know your name."

Miss Murdock pinked a little. "My goodness but I'm thick. I'm Gertrude Murdock, Mr. Crowder's secretary." For some reason she was reluctant to mention Frazer's name. "Another official saw the manuscripts and asked me in to read them. I never read anything like them and yet they are all different. Now, what do you say?"

Marvelle shrugged helplessly. "I can't believe it. I don't know anything to say."

"Well. do you agree with what I've said?"

"You mean about the agent?"

"Yes."

"You know what you're talking about, Miss Murdock. I certainly don't know anything about the writing business and this is the first I even knew about my talent ... if any."

"Didn't you do well in composition in school?"

"Very well, but I never thought of it commercially. My teacher always liked my style and I suppose it was she who put the commercial angle in my mind. But believe me, I had forgotten I'd sent the stuff to Crowder's. I did it just to have something to do and really, I suppose I may have had some dim motive like seeing just how an editor would react ... something like that."

"Well," said Miss Murdock crisply, "you've hit and you've hit big."

"You sound very sure."

"I'll tell you one thing. If Crowder's doesn't take your stories and at least try to put you under exclusive contract, then I'll resign and take up cats, parrots and tattooing."

Marvelle squeezed her face between her hands. "It's so ... I just can't believe it. Me, a writer and selling to Crowder's ... My teacher used to say in a faintly ironical tone that it was the ambition of every writer since nineteen hundred to someday publish in Crowder's."

Miss Murdock chuckled. "I can support that. Our slush pile is enormous and for every one that is accepted, thousands go back."

"Slush pile?"

"That's where all unsolicited manuscripts go first. We read them religiously because once in a blue moon ... yours, for instance, we find something worthwhile."

"But you said an official saw them."

"So I did. I'll tell you about it. Right now we have more important things to do, like breakfast." She stopped and frowned.

"Breakfast. Ah yes. That'd be just the bait for that insatiable little monster ... Bern Wolff. For my money, he's the best agent in New York. He's crusty, with a hard veneer, but he's really fine. deep down. He has a cruel tongue and will probably make you furious at him once a day. Just the same, he's the man for you."

She picked up the phone and dialed rapidly. "Bern, this is Gert Murdock. We're having hot muffins, fresh salmon steaks broiled with bacon and butter..." The phone made squawky protesting noises and Miss Murdock hung up, her sharp angular face alight with a grin. "He can't resist food and he says I'm the best cook in New York."

Bern Wolff was not exactly a shock to Marvelle but he looked far different from her picture of a dashing, fast-talking agent. He slouched into the apartment, his hand in the pockets of his rumpled jacket that was clean but looked slept in. He stopped when he saw Marvelle dressed now in a smoothly fitting dress of lavender orlon which Miss Murdock had brought along the night before. Her hair was combed straight back and frothed on either side of her neck in twin ponytails. He glared at her for a moment, gnawing on his bottom lip.

"Quit staring, Bern," snapped Miss Murdock coming into the living room. "This is Marvelle Martingale ... Bern Wolff."

He lifted a long fingered hand and silenced her. "Please wait until I get through resenting her. This is no time of day to encounter a visitation. I've not had my coffee. Martingale ... Hell, I ..."

"Please be silent, Bern," barked Miss Murdock with such vehemence that he threw a swift look at her.

"Now, breakfast all."

Marvelle had never eaten fish for breakfast before, but she did complete justice to her salmon, muffins and coffee. "I didn't know fish could be so good," she said, her eyes shining with appreciation.

"You," said Wolff slowly, "probably come from a part of the country where the only way to cook fish is rolling it in flour or crumbs and frying it in deep grease." He shuddered. "Gert here has no such sadistic approach to good food."

After breakfast, Miss Murdock served more coffee. "While you drink your coffee," she told him, "I have something I want you to read."

He looked at her sourly. "I know. Some panting protege has penned the long lost short story. The ultimate, the pinnacle."

"Shut up and read," she said savagely, shoving the manuscripts at him. He looked at the name, glanced enigmatically at the girl and began to read swiftly. Two paragraphs later he had slowed perceptibly. From there on he read with extreme care and concrete concentration. When he finished, he looked at Marvelle. "If you tell em you wrote this, I very much fear I must call you a liar."

She laughed, feeling free and exuberant. "I wrote it. I suppose in forty minutes. Maybe an hour."

His pugnacious countenance darkened. "I must tell you. I hate people who can write fast. I'm a plodder myself." He looked at Miss Murdock. "I suppose you got me up here to foist this kid off on me?"

Miss Murdock pursued her thin lips. "You've read the first one. What do you think?"

He sighed and shook his head. "There's something wrong here. I won't knit. Is this the stuff that turned up yesterday in the slush pile?"

She saw he had caught her warning about mentioning Frazer's name. "Yes," she said. "I was asked to read them. I did. You haven't told me what you think?"

He took a deep breath and fumbled for a cigarette. He lit it and inhaled a searing cloud of smoke. He nodded slowly. "What do I think? I think..." He lifted his head and looked at the girl. "You don't lie very easily. Again, I ask you. Did you write this?"

"Yes sir,"

"Never mind the sir. I know you're a few years younger than me. Don't rub it in. I'm still resenting you and I hate fast writers." He looked at Miss Murdock. "Do you believe her?"

"Certainly, I believe her. I saw material by the stacks in her apartment."

He shook his head and sighed again. "All right. I guess I'll go along for the ride. Kid, do you have an agent?"

"No. Miss Murdock and I are hoping you'll agree to handle me."

He pulled out a contract form. "This is the deal. Read it and we'll get legal as all hell. When you sign it, I've got you. The usual ten percent and fringe benefits."

Marvelle read the contract. It seemed very fair and reasonable to her, but she had always had an aversion to signing anything binding. She handed it back. "I'm afraid I can't sign it, Mr. Wolff."

He swallowed and inhaled more smoke. "Why not?"

"I just don't like contracts. I'll agree to everything in it, though."

He did an obvious double take. "Well, that's thoughtful of you, but what do I have as assurance?"

"My word. I solemnly swear to abide by the provisions of the contract. I don't think you'd cheat me and I certainly would not cheat you."

He looked at her a long time then turned to Miss Murdock with a sour grin. "The silly part is, she means it."

"Yes," said Miss Murdock who had just seen something very beautiful. "She means it. When have you heard something like that, Bern...as convincing, sincere?"

"Never," he muttered. "All right, kid. I have your word but I don't have any marbles. I'll take you on that basis with one provision."

"What's that?"

"That you pinch me every so often so I can be damn sure that marbles or no, I'm still Bern Wolff."

Marvelle laughed delightedly. "Miss Murdock, I think I'm going to like Mr. Wolff."

"Cheers," he said hollowly.

Miss Murdock, still enthralled with the beauty she had discovered, a person who gave her word with the solidity and profundity of a notarized statement. "He's a nasty little man," she said, "it won't be necessary to like him."

"And," Bern broke in, "this little man has work to do." He turned to Marvelle. "They'll want an interview. They'll want you on an exclusive contract. That's not usual but neither are you. What'll you do about that?"

"I won't sign it," she said

"Oh dear," said Miss Murdock.

"Now that's a mixed contract I can go along with and I will. Gert you taking her in today?"

"With me ... yes."

"All right. I'll go home and ... When do you leave here?"

"Eight-thirty."

"All right. I'll meet you two in the lobby. I want to brief my girl before we get there." He stood up and thrust his hands into his jacket pockets. "Gert, this kid throws me. I'm excited and sort of scared."

It was Marvelle's time for a double take. "Whatever for, Mr. Wolff?"

"Please call me Bern." He frowned hideously. "Because I feel I have a tiger by the tail, that's why. Nothing about this whole silly thing is right. You're too beautiful and in some magic way you have the talent for transferring that beauty to the written word on paper. I don't even mean that entirely. I don't know what I mean ... just that I never read anything that got me in the wishbone like that thing did. I'll take the others and read them while walking down the street." He turned abruptly and walked out.

Marvelle hugged herself and her skin prickled all over. "Miss Murdock, I think I'm afraid too."

Miss Murdock cleared the dishes and chuckled. "Of what, child?"

"Oh…everything. It's such a shock…so strange. All of a sudden I just feel shaky all over."

"It'll pass," said the older woman. "I guess I know what you mean, though. You see, a good many people in the publishing business are would-be writers. Many never get past the stage of telling themselves that they could equal half what they see in print. Stay as you are. Write as you always have and I can't see a stopping point for you. There's nothing that can stop you. I gathered from the fluid style, the ease with which you write and the speed that you are a subconscious writer. Am I correct?"

"Yes. I write for release from something, I guess. I'm afraid I couldn't do very well if I had to consciously think everything out, make an outline and things like that. I'm never well enough acquainted with a character at the beginning of a story to be able to project very well what he'll do at the end of it. By the way, I've started a novel."

"Oh…how is it going?"

"Very well, I suppose. I don't seem to be having any trouble with it. It comes out as easily as my shorter stuff."

"I suppose around a hundred or so pages.

"Then stay with it. From that pile of stuff I saw at your place, you're way ahead on the short stuff."

Wolff joined them in the lobby, his eyes half slitted against the smoke from the cigarette that hung limply in one corner of his mouth. He didn't speak but followed them to the street where he hailed a cab and opened the door for them. He got in. "Grand Central Palace," he told the driver. "Four eighty Lexington, entrance."

For a full two minutes Wolff scowled at the floor then turned to the girl. "You're serious about that contract?"

"You mean with Crowder's?"

"Yes."

"I am."

"All right. I'll tell you why I agree. Those contracts were designed for valuable writers who slave and knock themselves silly and go through all the pains of childbirth to dig a story out of their systems. Then they spend days even months editing, polishing, rewriting... tearing themselves to bits over it. In that way their output can't be very high. With you... suppose you dumped twenty short stories like these three in their laps. They'd die by degrees but they couldn't publish all of them. Under contract you couldn't sell what they didn't take to anyone else. That's why I say for you, no contract. They'll get mad and puff and blow, but if they don't want you under your own terms, then I can name you half a dozen outfits that'll jump at you."

"This is treason," snapped Miss Murdock.

He grinned lopsidedly. "So was siccing me onto her before the interview. We've signed our verbal contract and Crowder's will have to sing for their material."

Marvelle frowned slightly. "This is all very well but everyone seems to forget, they haven't accepted anything yet."

Wolff nodded. "So they haven't. Gert and I've been in this business too long not to know a find when we see one. They'll accept your material."

"*He,*" said Miss Murdock guardedly, "hasn't even read them yet... the coward."

"*He,*" replied Wolff, "has instinct. He doesn't have to be smart. He was wise to get you to look at them first."

"He'll have to read them, though," she said. "Today."

"He's a fast reader. It won't take any time."

Marvelle was not prepared to see Craine Frazer and when they walked into his office, she uttered a little cry and turned to run, barging into Bern and knocking him sprawling. As Miss Murdock caught her, she had a lurid fit of hysterics. Miss Murdock wrestled her into a chair and slapped her resoundingly, making her cries subside into convulsive sobbing.

She released the girl and stood straight. "You can probably handle this better alone. Buzz me in Crowder's office when you want us back."

Frazer was stretched to the point of distraction himself. "Stay here, Gert," he ordered sharply. Wolff, however, went out. Frazer wrung his slender fingers nervously.

"Marvelle, what happened?"

She looked up, her face charged with misery. "I didn't expect...you. I didn't know...you were here." She wept bitterly for a while. "I know what you must think of me and...you're right. Maybe I shouldn't care what you think. You're nothing to me. But I do care. I don't know why and when I see you I just curl up and want to die." She got up. "I'll go now."

"No." he said with harsh positiveness. "This is a business meeting and I'm not the captain of your soul. I'm not sitting in judgment. I didn't want to read it myself because I was afraid I'd be prejudiced in your favor. I wanted other opinions. You came in with Bern Wolff so he must be handling you."

"I...agreed to let him handle me this morning."

"All right. Let's try to keep personalities out of this. I have every respect for Miss Murdock's judgment...Did Bern read your stuff?"

"Yes. He liked it."

"That's an understatement. For him to take on an unknown at a moment's notice means only one thing. He read your material and it flattened him. He's not easy to impress either. Now I'm going to get him back in here if you're feeling better."

When Wolff arrived, Marvelle was under taut control but she huddled in the chair silently and would look at no one.

Frazer looked sharply at the agent. "Miss Martingale and I know each other. Recently she has been under a strain and what with the shock of seeing me here, unexpectedly, and the even greater shock of impressing two severe critics the first time she ever submitted anything, was a combination she couldn't weather. I think she'll be all right now."

Wolff mouthed a cigarette out of the way of speech and said, "All right. suppose I show my girl the place while you read her stuff. Time is of the essence and if you don't want her then I know someone who does. Come on, kid. I'll show you the place." She followed him out, repressing a desire to kiss this strange little man who acted so hard but whose sensitivity was exquisite. Wolff realized that she needed time to gather her wits and recover from shock. He realized that Frazer had spoken for effect and not from fact. He remembered, too, the sketchy remarks Frazer had made about her magnetism, her alcoholism. He shrugged his shoulders hard. It was impossible to believe that this fresh unspoiled girl could be so afflicted but he knew Frazer was not a liar.

Frazer was discovering that his original impulse not to read Marvelle's work had been well grounded. Her technique had a rushing breathless quality that in some manner communicated itself to the reader. Her word choice was uninhibited and so natural that there was not a hint of labor to her phraseology. She had something to say. She said it fluidly, fast but with an impact that had his back aching from the strain when he finished. He was too intelligent not to realize that some of his tension was because he knew her. His problem was how much and where was it located. He did not know and he doubted if he ever would. Crowder's would have to have her. It would be the rankest stupidity to let someone like Gaffer of Cosmos Publications get. a chance at her.

Frazer frowned for a long moment then buzzed the executive vice president. "Sutton. I have something here that's as hot as a Bikini fallout. I'd like to talk to you about it because the author should be under contract. We stand to lose the best prospect I've seen since I've been here if we don't strike and strike hard."

Sutton's rich smooth voice came back. "Sure, Craine. Be down in a minute."

"Forget I was here?" snapped Miss Murdock from her chair behind Frazer.

He started. He had forgotten she was there. He grinned. "Yes, I'd forgotten."

"Want to tell me why or shall I tell you?"

"You've been right on all counts, Gert. I think Sutton ought to be in on this."

"It must be serious if you want to bring him in."

He nodded. "It's serious all right." He bit his lower lip. "We've got the hottest property I've seen yet and I'm not sure what we're to do with it. We can't overload on her stuff and yet these stories of hers make me want to stop the presses and tear out just about anything they have set up and run hers instead."

"I'd do it anyhow. That baseball story by John McArthur ... it's all right but that's about all I can say for it."

"It's time to run a baseball story."

"Sure and if it hadn't been time to run one you wouldn't have had 'Home Run Home' as a gift. Be honest, Longhorn."

He laughed. "All right. Tell Morgan to pull it and run 'Marlene' by Marvelle Martingale."

"With pleasure."

"Reckon Sutton will agree?"

"To what?" asked the big florid man as he walked in. He had thin white hair, predatory eyes and thick sensual lips.

"This," said Frazer handing him the manuscript. "We've located something that's almost too hot to hold. If you don't believe it when you read it ... I didn't believe it either."

"What he means," put in Miss Murdock, "is you won't believe that a nineteen-year-old girl did it, two others that we've read and a roomful of them at her place. He means we've got to get her on contract and fast."

"Ummm," said Sutton shifting his cigar. "Let's see what this paragon has done."

He read the story with the quick all-seeing eye of an experienced editor. Once he glanced up at them accusingly but the rest of the time he read with deep concentration. Finally he looked up and handed it back to Farzer. "Did you say a nineteen-year-old?"

Frazer shook his head. "Gert said it. I concur."

Sutton sighed seismically. "Things like this always make me uncomfortable. It puts us in a position we don't often occupy and when we do I feel uncomfortable. I hate to go out after a writer. It puts them in too good a position."

"I take it," said Miss Murdock, "that you like the story."

Sutton gnawed at his cigar. "As you know, I'm averse to superlatives. I like her and we have to have her. That's all I have to say. Can we squeeze her into the next issue?"

"Yes, if we can pull the baseball story," replied Frazer.

"Do it, by all means ... by *all* means. Every issue we print without her the later she gets to the public eye. When that happens ..." He shrugged. "We'd best get set because we're going to be in for some high times. Who found this kid?"

Frazer grinned. "I guess it's a four way thing. Elaine dropped the stories accidentally from the pile of slush. Bern Wolff picked it up and commented on her name. I recognized the name and asked Gert here to read it. Actually. Gert discovered her."

"Good for Gert. Now, has she been contacted?"

"Yes. She's in the building."

"Where?"

"Bern Wolff is showing her around."

Sutton groaned and caught his head in both hands. "Ye gods, she's in the hands of the worst Philistine of all. He'll bleed us white and we'll have to take it."

"That should be a salutary experience," commented Miss Murdock acidly. "You never suffered when you got material for peanuts."

He looked at her severely. "Miss Murdock, our price for good shorts is seven-fifty and has been for some time." "I know, but that's since you crawled up the ladder. I haven't forgotten what you paid when you worked for *Love Lorn* because I sent you stuff."

He flushed. "I'd just as soon you'd forget those days."

"I'm sure … well, here comes the Philistine with our treasure."

Marvelle felt a great deal better now. Her brisk tour had flushed her face slightly and her eyes sparkled.

"Miss Martingale, Mr. Sutton." growled Wolff in mock bad temper. 'He's Crowder's without the name."

"How do you do," she said sweetly, giving him her most scintillant smile. Mr. Sutton recoiled slightly as though she had struck him … as indeed she had. He gulped and made a peeping noise, gruffed savagely and forced a greeting. After his first flounder, he recovered and said, "I will get to the point. Miss Martingale. We think a great deal of your style. We like your work and we want to print it, but we'd like to have you under contract. You're too valuable for us to run any risk with you."

Wolff grunted, took a chair and chewed his cigarette into the corner of his mouth where it hung limply. "Get ready to catch the pieces, Gert," he said and cut a hard look at Sutton's face.

Sutton glared at him then back to the girl. "We'll accept your submissions and our going rate is seven-fifty. That satisfactory to you?"

"If you mean seven-fifty in hundreds … yes."

Wolff straightened up. "Don't talk so fast. I can get you more."

She shook her head. "I'm not asking for special treatment. I feel that seven-fifty would be all right."

"In other words," said Wolff, "you've given your word."

"That's right. I agreed. I couldn't go back on that now."

"Hah," bared Mr. Sutton triumphantly. "I'm glad to know there are people in the world whose word is still good." He got up and pressed her hand warmly. "Miss Martingale, I can see that it will be a holiday of pleasures to do business with you."

Wolff grinned sourly. "Better not crow too soon, Sutton. What was it you were saying about contracts?"

"Ah ... yes, of course. Miss Martingale, I offer you a contract. which means that we'll contract for your entire output at our regular price. Naturally we reserve the right to reject material unsuited to our uses."

She looked him straight in the eyes. "How many stories of mine can you use in a year?"

He shifted uncomfortably. He didn't like the question any better than most editors. "We should be able to use one an issue, but of course that would be an impossible strain upon you. Also we'd have to use a nom de plume if we did that. We wouldn't want to flood the market with your name so as to make a nuisance value of it."

"She could write a year's supply for you in a week," commented Wolff, "so don't strain your concern. We take it that those manuscripts you turn down we'd be free to peddle."

Sutton looked apoplectic. "A year's supply in a week?"

"Maybe I overstated that," said Wolff. "She has a year's supply already written. I'd forgotten for a moment that you were a weekly."

Sutton recovered with an effort. Things had been going a little too fast for him. "Now about the contract..." He looked hotly at Wolff. "Of course you won't be allowed to peddle her other stuff around. Her style would be recognized... What do you think a contract is for?"

"There'll be no contract, Mr. Sutton," she said firmly.

Sutton gulped and swallowed. "No ... contract?"

"Why?" asked Frazer harshly.

She turned to him. "Mr. Frazer, I have a great deal to be thankful for that is directly related to you, but I will not sign a contract with Crowder's."

"If they get hard about," said Wolff with a crooked grin, "I can get you in at Cosmos without half trying."

JOHN BURTON THOMPSON

"Mr. Wolff, please be silent," snapped Mr. Sutton, his face turkey red. "Miss Martingale what is your objection to a contract?"

"My objection is that you will not be able to handle my output. Why, therefore, shouldn't I be able to see my stuff elsewhere, that of it you don't want to use? Naturally, I'd give you first look. I'd even agree to show you my novel first with possible serialization in view. I'll give you all the material you can use. What do you want with a contract?"

"I'll tell you," said Wolff, "because even though he might try, he'd never quite get around to it. Everyone in this room with the exception of your lovely self has suddenly come to realize that if you're not the sensation of the year then none of us knows publishing and should peddle brushes or cheap perfume. Crowder's being no greater hog than Cosmos or any other magazine ... but a hog withal, wants sole ownership. Understandable in the peculiar philosophy of Wall Street and the publishing marts, but hardly the handiest thing for the poor scrivener who still feeds off crumbs unless he has what it takes to demand and get a piece of virgin cake."

Sutton made helpless motions with his hands. "How do we know, Miss Martingale, that we'll get first look at your stuff? We're putting you before the American public. We merely want to protect our investment."

"I told you I'd give you first look. You have my word."

"I seem to remember," said Wolff drily, "a moment ago you were praising the sterling quality of her word. The quality hasn't depreciated."

"But ... but ... This is unthinkable. It makes for an intolerable situation." He frowned. "How is it that you who have such an aversion for contracts are being handled by Mr. Wolff?"

"Oh but we have a contract," said Wolff.

"Ah," growled Sutton, "then I fail to see ..."

"You fail to see a lot," put in Miss Murdock. "Their contract is a verbal agreement. The signature is her word."

Mr. Sutton having known the agent for a long time, made a strangling sound. "You mean you took her word ..."

"Just so," said Wolff easily. "Now you know how I felt earlier this morning when I handed her a contract and got it back in the mush. She says you'll get first look You'll get it. You have no right to tie up her entire output when you can't use even a fraction of it."

Frazer looked deflated but not as much as Sutton. Frazer was angry at something but he was not sure what it was. Maybe the intimation by the girl that she thought he might consider that doing her favors was a reason for her to agree to their contract suggestion.

Miss Murdock said, "I can't see what you figure to lose. She stands to lose a great deal if you wrap her up in a contract."

Marvelle, whose nerves were not of the best and who was tasting the heady wine of success, picked up her material abruptly from Frazer's desk. "Let's go, Mr. Wolff. Apparently Crowder's wants to swallow more than they can digest."

Wolff got up but Sutton was ahead of him. "Now ... now, just a moment. If the young lady is allergic to contracts, then I think maybe we can work out something else."

"I think you can, too," said Miss Murdock, caustically.

CHAPTER ELEVEN

The word, as might have been expected, had gotten out and Marvelle was not prepared for it. It is not an easy thing to be transported in one day from the dim grottoes of obscurity into a name that sets New York agog.

The first panting reporter met Wolff and the girl as they emerged from the Palace and wanted to get the scoop.

"I'm Dawson of *'Broadway Beat.'* What's this about the girl prodigy, Wolff?"

The agent scowled and drove his fists deeper into his jacket pockets, giving his shoulders a skinned look. "I have her, she'll be a prodigy, she's with Crowder's and the sky's the limit. That's all for now. If you want the details, see Hutchins in my office."

"I've come from there. He doesn't know from because."

"He will tomorrow. My client is tired. Good day."

He whisked her into a cab and gave directions after asking Marvelle her address. "About time for a late lunch, isn't it?"

She nodded. "Mr. Wolff, you know about my trouble, I suppose."

"You mean with the bottle?"

"Yes, and what a beast I am when I'm drinking."

"Yes and no. I know some details of your trouble but you're money in my pocket and I'm not your priest. Tell me anything you want to and not a word that you want to keep to yourself. I'm here to take all the bumps off you I can. You're going to be the toast of the town and it'll confuse you. It'll make you nervous. It'll make you dizzy. Take what you want of it. Tell me what you

don't like and I'll steer you around it. I might even get propri-
etary and start maneuvering you. If I do, it'll be because I see you
don't know where to go."

She sighed comfortably and tried to still her jumpy nerves.
"It's all so sudden and strange. You're being so good to me that I
feel all watery inside."

"Don't try to make an angel out of me," he said harshly. I'm
a hardheaded business man. I'm trying to protect my client and
make her like me at the same time."

"And," she said with a tremulous smile, "you're succeeding
marvelously. I don't know what I'd do without you."

"Quite well, probably," he replied. "Agents like to think that
no writer can succeed without them. It's an occupational psy-
chosis. In your case, I'm glad to say, I can help because you are so
profoundly stupid."

She laughed. "You're the only man who ever said that to me
and made me like it."

He turned his cynical eyes to her and examined her for a
moment. "Thanks. You've sense, bottom and guts. You knew
what I meant and didn't throw a hypersensitive tizzy. You're all
right. That's what I'm for but I like the way you handled the situation in Frazer's office. You'll learn fast, then you won't need me."

"I doubt that," she said earnestly. "I felt you were there support-
ing me in Mr. Frazer's office. That's why I was as good as I was."

"I was with you all the way. I even agree about the price. I
have a profound respect for personal ethics. I admit that to
you because anyone else would be tempted to give me a loud
horselaugh."

She placed a cool soft hand on his arm. "Then they'd be
silly. They'd say that because you appear so hard and yet I know
you're not."

Wolff flushed. He disliked having people see beneath his
crusty exterior. "That's something you can see because I'm soft
where you're concerned. It isn't an everyday thing."

"You're a bad liar, Mr. Wolff."

"If you don't mind, I'm going to be around for a while. Please call me Bern or something."

They stopped at a small restaurant and ate baked beans and knockwurst. Bern washed his down with beer and she drank milk. When they got to her apartment, the entrance was swarming with reporters. He paid off the taxi and stood glowering at them for a moment.

"I doubt that any of them know you. They know me. I'll go up and engage them in conversation. When I have their attention, slip by and go to your apartment. I'll be up after a while...as soon as I get rid of them." He stopped and made a wry face. "That's Wolff for you. I asked myself up, didn't I? Well, forget it. I'll see you tomorrow."

She put her hand on his arm. "No, I want you to come up. There is so much to talk about and yet I can't think of a thing right at the moment."

He nodded. "I guess I must have known it without thinking about it. I'll be up."

As she opened her door the phone was ringing insistently. She hesitated for a moment, then tossed her soft hair with a resentful twist of her head, hardened her face and answered. It was Larsen.

For a moment she let the picture of him and the touch of his voice flow all over her, then tested it for reaction. There was none.

"I'm very glad to hear of your success, Marvelle. I wanted to call and let you know that. I don't think it could happen to a finer person."

"You don't really mean that, Dan," she said crisply. "However, I thank you for the thought."

"But I do mean it. Really I do."

"No. You and I know that this call was an impulse, a generous one, perhaps, but just an impulse. No one remembering

Walter Campbell and me that night in Westchester could think of me as a fine person. That's not your fault, of course."

He choked at the other end. "I'd nearly forgotten that, Marvelle."

"Until you'd need the memory. You can't forget it any more than I can. Good night, Dan, and thanks for calling."

She hung up and frowned at the wall. Only the thought of Wolff coming up soon kept her from the bottle. It struck her with force as soon as she hung up the phone. Was it a residue from her association with Larsen? Was it a cry in the night for the wonderful love they had made? Her body cried out now...cried out in a loud healthy voice for relief. Desire ripped her in a swift viscid tide that weakened her and dropped her on the couch. The phone rang again. Her face hardened again and her lips thinned. Whoever it was, she had had enough. She'd tell the operator in the lobby to stop all her calls.

She picked up the receiver and recognized the bleat of Edward Colton. "Marvelle. it's really marvelous ... I heard about your success. I'm so glad for you. Could I come around and talk about it? Really, you have no idea how the word is going around...surely you won't mind sharing your success with...I mean, wouldn't you like to talk about it to someone...?"

"Colt, I've told you before. I'll tell you again, stop bothering me. You don't want to talk about my success...honest now do you?"

His groan was answer enough. "Marvelle, after what we had...you mean there's nothing...nothing at all? Please let me see you, let me talk to you. Like I told you before...anything...anything at all. I'll marry you and spend my life being your slave."

She uttered a coarse word. "Colt, you're getting corny as hell. What show did you pick up that mossy line from? Goodbye."

She hung up fuming, wondering why his babbling always annoyed her. Larsen did not make her heart beat faster and they had had a great deal more than she and Colton had ever achieved. Still Larsen didn't annoy her as did Colton. The bottle was at her lips and halfway through the first long drink when she realized what she had done. She took it down, eyed it combatively. then perversely took another one, then a third. before she put the bottle down. She looked around for disapproval. feeling that she'd slaughter it in some irresistible fashion. She saw it in Wolff's deep-sunken. brow-shaded eyes as he stood inside the doorway.

"What's that for?" he asked coldly.

She collapsed on the couch and wept bitterly. "Maybe you'd better just forget about me," she said between sobs. "I'm no good, Bern. I let an old flame anger me into doing that and if it hadn't been him, it would have been something or someone else."

He stared at her for a moment. "You know, if I'm going to be your agent, I ought to know what makes you perk. Have another drink."

She sat up and stared at him. "You mean it?"

"You've started anyway and I didn't start you. Believe me, I just want to observe you."

She was vastly relieved. The fever in her loins had approached the danger point. If she were in a bar now, she'd begin looking for a likely man. Four drinks further along and it'd be any man. She wondered if he was a good lover and almost without trying, her facile mind began to plot. She did not know that most alcoholics have similarly facile minds as long as they have minds at all. She rolled over sinuously and the amount of thigh that her skirt revealed made his mouth go dry. He shrank within and an iron resolve grew into being.

"Shall I fix you one?"

"Of course."

They sat on the couch. He sipped his drink, she gulped hers at a ratio of two to one. His resolve held and it began to annoy her. Suddenly she flopped into his arms, her own around his neck, her fabulous mouth seeking and finding his.

It was a smothering, devouring kiss and though he could not resist the maddening attack, he still retained an icy inner composure. She raved and twisted and fought him...fought herself against him, rapidly losing anything that might resemble balance until at last she was crying and begging him in piteous tones to give her release from the dragon that was devouring her from within. He tore her arms from him and slid from the couch. In a matter of seconds it seemed she was out of her clothes and back she came begging, entreating...with words, with the poetic magnificence of her body, so smooth and hot to the touch, that his composure was strained to the limit. He held her at arms length, staring with horrified calm at her twisted passion-blasted face, then with regret he smashed her on the chin with his fist. She crumpled to the carpet and spread out...even in unconsciousness so ineffably graceful and lovely that tears stung the cynical eyes. He turned and stumbled away, his eyes looking, searching for something that might his eyes looking, searching for something that might suggest something else. He found her purse and he began to search or something...a sedative, some medication that she might be carrying...anything.

He found a card and pounced upon it. He studied the penciled number since it seemed to be a residential number and since it was after the hour when an office would likely to be open, he dialed the number.

A strong resonant voice answered. "Dr. Leibermann speaking."

"Doctor, I found your card in a girl's purse. She's rather in a state and since you've treated her, I thought you wouldn't mind making a house visit. She's in no condition to visit you."

"What's her name?"

"Marvelle Martingale."

"Ah … the lovely Marvelle. Luckily I do remember her and I told her to call any time."

"Well, she's past calling anyone. Will you come?"

"Yes. Right away. Who're you?"

"Bern Wolff. I'm Miss Martingale's literary agent."

"I was not aware that she wrote … oh, she mentioned something about it, but I thought it was just a hobby of sorts."

"Until today it was. I'll tell you about it." The agent gave Dr. Leibermann the address and hung up. He picked her from the floor, strong for all his slight build, and took her into the bedroom. He searched and failed to find anything that suggested a night dress. No pajamas, no gown … nothing. He compromised with a robe. getting it on her with considerable difficulty. The exorbitant magnificence of her body jangled and prodded his consciousness, no matter how hard he tried to ignore it. and more than once he was forced to remind himself forcibly of his resolve.

He had hardly gotten her tucked away when he heard the doorbell ring. He took a last heart-sick look at the small red swelling on her chin and went out.

Aaron Leibermann towered over Wolff by a head and a half. He was well dressed and very assured. "You're Wolff?"

"Yes. I suppose you're the doctor." They shook hands.

"Now what's with my patient?"

"I had to tap her on the chin. She got drunk, then she got amorous."

"Some would consider that a rather ideal situation."

"I suppose some would. Instead, I called you. I'd taken all I could. I'm not stone, you know."

"I don't think it would have made much difference if you had been," said the doctor, shaking his head. "I hadn't heard from her and was about to do something very unprofessional by calling her. Where is she?"

"In the bedroom. I managed to get a robe on her."

"Let's see her."

They went into the bedroom where the doctor took her pulse, took out a small sphygmomanometer and took her blood pressure. He pulled her robe aside and listened to her heart, trying to keep his eyes from the firm solid hillocks of creamy pink-tipped flesh that sprang so proudly from her chest. He sighed and put his instruments away. "I can find nothing wrong. She's tight, I suppose, and it was easy to knock her out. Did you hit her hard?"

"No," said Wolff tightly. "I hit her as easy as I could... but instead of catching her, I watched her fall to the carpet like I was a zombie or something."

"Understandable in this case. Miss Martingale is a very upsetting collection of feminine attraction." He cut a cutting glance at the agent. "You say you called me instead of doing what she wanted?"

"That's what I said."

"Then I must compliment you... or feel sorry for you. I don't know which."

"I can do without any reaction from you whatever," snarled Wolff harshly. "I'm as human as you or anyone else, but I've never taken advantage of a drunk, sick girl and I never will. It doesn't matter a good damn how beautiful she is."

"Softly, friend. softly. You are, of course, right, and I have no right suspecting you. I apologize."

"The hell with that. What'll you do?"

"Revive her first. Let her talk if she will then give her a non-barbiturate sleeping dose."

"Why non-barbiturate?"

"Barbiturates and alcohol have an unfortunate affinity. A synergistic action which is more profound than either would produce alone. There is danger in giving both. However, I have something in my bag that will suffice."

The shock of the blow had effectively driven the hungry hysteria from the girl and when she was revived, she wept hard for a while then Wolff said roughly, "All right, dammit, turn off the shower and listen to the doctor."

She gasped and looked at him through startled eyes, then at the doctor. "It was really wonderful of you to come, Dr. Leibermann."

"I said I would and I'm here. What triggered it off tonight."

She shrugged helplessly. "It seems I can write. I didn't dream it would be what it seems. It was a shock. I saw Frazer ... he's an editor at Crowder's. I didn't expect to see him. From this morning when I woke up in Miss Murdock's apartment till late this afternoon, there has been one shock after another. My success has blown all over the city like wildfire. Reporters had my door besieged when I got home. Mr. Wolff got me by them, all right, but then when I got inside my door the phone began to ring. First Larsen, then Colton. My whole past ... from the time I arrived in New York seemed to rise up and ..." She shook her head. "I just reached for the bottle automatically."

"You needn't reach now," said Wolff morosely. "I poured it down the drain."

"Then," said the girl flushing with shame, "I threw myself at Mr. Wolff until he had to slug me on the chin." She gagged, sobbed, and went into another fit of weeping.

"I'm going to give you a shot" said Dr. Leibermann gently. "You'll have a good natural sleep and tomorrow will turn out to be another day."

"I'm afraid of tomorrows, now," she whispered.

"Nonsense. You're a new success and the city will be clamoring for you. Television, interviews, offers. Hollywood will be knocking, the world at your feet."

She shuddered. "I'm afraid of all that. I don't want to be sought after and in demand."

Leibermann sighed. "I suppose every success has its bumps. This time you followed advice and got drunk in your own apartment."

"Yes," she said bitterly, "and followed my usual habit of throwing myself at the first pair of pants I saw."

"That is scarcely a compliment," said Wolff crabbily, "but I'd advise against it in the future. Even this poorly stuffed pair of pants has its limits."

Her face went soft with heart-aching contrition. "Please, Bern … I didn't mean it that way."

He grinned crookedly. Better get along with the needle, Doctor. She'll have a full day tomorrow, likely."

She looked at Wolff anxiously. "Please, Bern … will you stay with me? I'm all of a sudden afraid to be alone." She smiled tremulously. "And I know I'll be safe."

"Yes, dammit, you will. I'll stay."

Dr. Leibermann gave her a shot and stayed chatting freely about trivialities until her eyes grew heavy, then closed. He motioned to Bern and they went into the tiny living room. Dr. Leibermann sighed heavily. "Did you really pour the delightful fluid down the drain?"

"No." said the agent, "but it's an idea."

"I think it'd be a better idea if we drank it."

They sat in chairs facing the couch. Bern put his feet carelessly on the couch. "Your concern about my performance as it touches on our Marvelle, makes me suspect that you've had to look rather deeply into your own inner mirror where she's concerned."

Leibermann laughed shortly. "No man, not a fool, will make ponderous pronouncements as to what he'll do under provocation because no man is ever that well tested. No man has seen everything nor has he really known all manner of provocation. Sober and coldly objective he might be a paragon of resistance, although being a paragon of resistance merely for the sake of being strong is, to my notion, a very sterile ambition. Slightly tight or tighter than that, he might well become a slavering Casanova without an inhibition in the world. I recall once that we had a man in school who was the soul of sobriety, steady and...as you've guessed, rather dull. He was going to become a medical missionary. We teamed up on him one night and got him drunk on vodka and some aromatic mix so he wouldn't know what he was drinking, and turned another intern loose on him. She was an unbelievably lush blonde and turned out to be a magnificent surgeon, mainly, I think, because she was so totally moral that nothing interfered with application to her work."

"Not even her amorality?"

"Oddly enough, it didn't. She could give you a roll and go blind with ecstasy and in five minutes it might not have happened. Well, we turned her loose on him when he was ripe and brother, did he ever crawl out of that shell of his." Leibermann smiled. "There are probably a lot of dead savages on some lonely island that he would have saved along with their immortal souls. Once the vial had opened and the genie escaped, Smalley...that was his name, could never coax him back again. He just raged and floated around leading Smalley down this and that path by the nose."

Leibermann drained his glass. "I wouldn't wish it on my worst enemy and I wouldn't accept such a job for a mint, but it would be nice if you could stay with her...oh, on a semi-permanent basis and sort of lead her away from the bottle, keep her busy with interviews, TV appearances and such. I doubt that any director could think so little of his career as to turn down the possibility of having her on his show...I'm assuming she's as good as you say she is."

"She's good," said Wolff shortly. "As for putting up any sort of semi-permanent residence here, you need to see a psychiatrist. This might sound strange to you, but the feeling I have toward her is a strange one indeed.

"Suppose cold sober she approached you and made you believe that she wanted to share a bed with you above all people?"

"That would take some doing, what with her past. If, however, she did succeed, then I'm afraid I'd be no more noble than any man."

"Then I don't see what you have to lose staying and giving her a hand. Surely you see that she'll make money for you. Just how much depends on how stable she remains. You could look at it as a cold business investment."

Wolff wrung his long sensitive fingers. "Don't pile things up on me. Her success was no more shock to her than meeting her was to me. I have wild notions like chucking everything and making myself her personal servant."

Leibermann looked at him carefully. "I'm a psychiatrist, Wolff, and if I don't know something about people, I'm in the wrong business. I think such an arrangement would be ideal for you both. Unless she beats this drinking habit. It'll beat her and you'll be back where you were ... wherever that is."

Wolff's mouth twisted sourly. "Back shepherding erratic arrived writers, shepherding those who'd like to arrive, trying to find talent where there is none, trying to entice it outside when it's shy. I suppose Saint Peter must have asked himself at some time or other, 'Why do I stick to this gate watching kick.' Everyone seems to think his own particular racket stinks, but you couldn't blast him loose from it."

Liebermann got to his feet. "You'd better think it over. It's easy for me to believe that she's as good as you and Crowder's think because I had a lot of ebullient impulses rushing around without any place to go, only because she's beautiful. No one should be only *that* beautiful. You find yourself wondering if it's merely a beautiful skin tacked over a beautiful body and ... period. or ... and let's pray hard that she can *do* something with it."

Wolff looked up, his eyes were shadowed, inscrutable but burning. "Suppose you were available and you met her. You would naturally be knocked for a loop but suppose you knew her background. What would be your reaction to the way she has spread herself around?"

Leibermann cracked his knuckles with sudden, explosive force making Wolff wince. "What a question. How the hell do I know? The trouble with knowing too much about people is that you're too prone to get sore and throw it in their faces. I have an idea that any man she marries will know in some of the stark detail she can produce when she wants to, just what she has been and he'll have the opportunity to accept her or reject her in the full knowledge of what she is ... or rather has appeared to be. The first time he got in a rage or a jealous fit and threw it in her face, probably would be the last time and there he'd be ... wishing he was dead, that someone had cut out his tongue, cuddling the crepe-draped prospect of existing without her. You the happy prospect?"

"No, thank God, I'm not. It's Craine Frazer. He's nuts about her and I think she'd go for him but there is her past standing in the way. They'll be meeting all the time and whatever she does, he'll know about it. If the Wailing Wall is all it's cracked up to be, I wish I had it handy."

Leibermann grinned tightly. "Well, I'll be an interested spectator. Call me any time."

When the doctor had gone the little man went back to the bedroom and stared for a long time at the girl who in a last waking moment had slipped from the robe and now sprawled with the abandoned grace of a sleeping kitten on her bed. Her face didn't change but something inside what was Bern Wolff changed as he watched, then with a lighter tread he walked back to the living room and composed himself on the couch.

CHAPTER TWELVE

There was no sound of an explosion the next morning when Marvelle waked but it seemed that the following twelve hours marked the opening bellow of the day her world disintegrated and sent her tumbling and confused ... staggering and reeling, buffeted and beaten, bounding from one shock to another like a cue ball bounding from the cushion of a pool table. Balance and coherence came in fits and starts and Bern Wolff, standing in her wake or before, wherever he was most needed, knew that his charge would never weather the storm.

Nineteen-year-old girls didn't write stories such as Marvelle Martingale did. No one ever sold a first effort or a first time out to Crowder's. Anyone who wrote as she did should be plain and dowdy, shy, retiring ... the peekaboo type, a frightened mouse in the center of Times Square. She dazzled them, she made writers emote into their columns and television greats besieged her to be their guest. Unknown guests ... relatively that is, are never offered princely sums of money, but she had been touched by the magic wand and caught the fancy of the most gullible city on earth.

She couldn't pay for a dress, a pair of stockings, a pair of briefs, a bra ... and to the horror of foundation manufacturers and their experts, refused to wear a girdle and often even a bra. Fabulous eating places threw open their doors and placed her where everyone on the establishment could see her.

No one was so coarse as to think of presenting a check. Her table was always laden with flowers and her new apartment atop the slender spire of the Huntingdon Tower reeked with layers of perfume from banks of the choicest product of the nation's florists.

Bravely she bore up, was warm and generous to everyone. Bravely she endured rapid questions and hollow jests, laughing at the proper time and smiling until her face ached as though she had an abscessed tooth ... then she began to fray and to Wolff's credit he realized it before she came to pieces. He would have called a halt sooner but he had a definite goal in mind. Let her swim with the tide, let her name become a household word and her face appear on the papers all over the nation. Let her become a familiar sight on magazine covers and in swim suits ... then he would pounce with his great idea. A series ... not a continued story, of her writing for television. Her show; just as many famous stars have their shows. She would introduce them and on occasions act in them. She had a studio test and they discovered that her natural simplicity was something many an actress achieved only after years of diligent work. With Marvelle, it was herself, so she was not conscious that she was acting at all.

Wolff did not take her through torturous channels but used his knowledge of his business to set up a conference with four or five of the industry's top men. They were almost convinced and after meeting her in person, they would be eating out of Wolff's hand. Of this he was certain, so he carefully made his plans.

For three weeks she had not had a drink. She lived from one excited moment to another and found a kind of compensation, a self-energizing stamina. She ate indifferently and when she went to bed, she collapsed in a dreamless coma that was tiring from its very profundity.

The morning arrived for the big conference and she was dressed in the simplest frock she owned, a single superbly fitted sheath that had the effect of being a spray of adornment rather than a dress. She seemed to be walking because she had somewhere to go.

It happened . . . the beginning of it, in the elevator going up to the fabled offices of a fabled maker and breaker of careers. The quietness seemed to batter down all her defenses. The long frenzy was gone suddenly and she felt a mighty orchestra of panic tuning up inside her, getting ready to smash the opening chord of the overture.

They left the elevator and she clung to his arm, trying to fight back the tide that was threatening to overwhelm her. They moved through a door that was opened for them into a softly lighted room. She never knew why, of the five men seated around the table talking in low voices, only one of them would remain in her memory. Wolff stopped for a moment just inside the room and surveyed them, allowed attention to shift and it was then that Marvelle looked into the most malign face she had ever seen. Columnists called Hunt Harrington's face saturnine. Trade papers called it purposeful. To her it was poison and his cold green eyes were those of a venomous snake. They settled on hers and their peculiar penetrating quality seemed to reach deep and triggered away what last reserve she had. She whirled like a cat and clung to Wolff screaming, *"Get me out of here . . . I can't stand it any longer . . . Please Bern . . Gel me out of here . . ."* He tried to soothe her but she was jerking and twitching on the verge of a convulsion.

"Calm the temperamental bitch and let's get on with it," came the cold measured tones of Hunt Harrington. Wolff turned hot fulminating eyes to the man and told him in measured gutter accents exactly what he was, where and from whom he had come, and suggested numerous paths of performance, none of which were acceptable to weak stomachs. Having relieved himself and feeling compensated for what they had probably lost, he turned, piloted her out of the room and slammed the door with a crash that satisfied his desire to rend and destroy.

A hurried telephone call had Dr. Leibermann waiting for them when the soundless elevator in Huntingdon Tower delivered them to the apartment.

She was shuddering and crying and to Wolff she didn't seem very well oriented. "She really flipped when we went in to see about the TV show," he said to Leibermann.

"She's a nervous wreck," said the doctor quietly. "Let's get her into bed."

The ordeal of getting the uncooperative lush-bodied girl into bed and beneath the covers had them both sweating before it was accomplished and little of their sweat was caused by heat ... not of the thermal variety, at any rate.

Liebermann gave her a snot and they restrained her gently until at last the barbiturate began to have effect. Her sobbing quieted and the convulsive movements became less. She looked sleepily at Wolff. "I'm terribly sorry I acted like I did, Bern. Terribly sorry."

"Forget it," he said gently. "They're a bunch of stuffed shirts. I was wrong. We should have made them come to us."

Her eyes widened as she remembered the terrible green eyes. "That many ... *his eyes* ..." She sobbed briefly, turned her head and gradually drifted off into a deep sleep.

Leibermann sighed gustily. "Whose eyes?"

"That illegitimate son of a bitch, Hunt Harrington, the Judas of the entertainment world. That excrescence that was dredged up out of some Bowery sewer."

"I've heard of him ... nothing good. He uses his position to fill his bed with the choicest of meat, makes and breaks men and women at a whim. That's the impression I've gathered."

"It's a good impression as far as it goes. If I'd known he was a partner in Bateman and Jones, I'd never have taken her there."

Leibermann cracked his fingers. "That man is a peculiar sort of animal. She's not free of him yet ... not if he took a shine to her."

Wolff's eyes were luminous. metallic. "That's one gal who'll never grace his bed. She was instantly repelled. That's what set her off, and I can see why. He's a savage without the heart of a pizza pie. I've heard a lot, of course, but I didn't really *know* until I saw him." Wolff chuckled without mirth. "I told him some things I never told any man. The bastard said, 'Calm the temperamental bitch and let's get on with it.'

"What makes you think he won't trim your sails, Wolff?"

Wolff's teeth bared in a snarl. "If Hunt Harrington stays put, then everything will be fine. I'd just as soon kill him as give him the time of day."

Leibermann was startled. "Look, fella, temper is one thing but..."

"Go on back to your office," said Wolff tiredly. "I'm bushed. How long will she sleep?"

"I hope about twenty hours. The shot along with her fatigue might make it go that long. She might wake sooner what with all the tension she's been under. What about her drinking?"

"She hasn't had a drink in three weeks."

"Sleep?"

"Not nearly enough and the wrong kind. She falls dead when she does sleep and doesn't move. She's staggering with weariness even when she wakes up."

"I shouldn't have to tell you, it's no good. She can't take it."

Wolff massaged his tired face. "I've been wrong about a lot of things. My idea was to burn the candle bright and hot while the world was looking then coast. Doc, there's no pinnacle she couldn't reach if she could stand the pace."

The doctor said an ugly word. "Maybe I'd better tell you something. There are better things than material success. She should relax and have a little quiet. When she does, she'll go back to the bottle as sure as you're alive."

Wolff nodded. "That's another reason why I've kept her busy...but as you say, she can't take it. I think I'll just call off the whole program. Writing is what she loves. She can make a fabulous living at just that. She doesn't need the world."

Leibermann wrung his long fingers. "She doesn't want the world. My knowledge of her is that she is a simple, uncomplicated small town girl who feels about like a salt water shad in a fish bowl. What you did with her was no more than natural but it's no good." Leibermann chuckled mirthlessly. "Neither is too much time for thought that leads her into tensions that leads her to the bottle. You've got to find the compromise. Something that will let her relax and rest without her mind running amok on her."

"I've got it," said Wolff. He tossed off a straight drink and lit a cigarette. "I've got just what you suggest, but I don't know how to use it."

"Tell me about it."

"It's Frazer, like I told you. He's what she needs. The problem is to remember that he observed her under some pretty disgusting conditions and how do you drive that from a man's mind?"

Leibermann smiled and poured another drink for himself. "You're going to have to become a psychiatrist and use tactics. See that they see a lot of each other. Arrange for them to be alone. Arrange for association whereby they will get to know each other well."

"Then what happens?"

"His residue of Victorianism will begin to shred away. He'll begin to dream up justification for her."

"Suppose she gets overheated and …"

"In that case we've got it beat. Once he gets a taste of what that girl can provide, then no amount of Victorianism can stand up. He'll have to go through the wringer, but something tells me you don't care how much he suffers as long as it gets the job done."

"I'd barbecue him if I thought it'd help," said the agent grimly. He looked up. "Maybe you know how I feel about this kid and maybe you don't. At first she as just a client, now it's something else entirely."

"In love with her, Wolff?"

"Yes, I think I am, but not in the usual way. Naturally, I've conceived a great personal affection for her. Physically she attracts me, but I'll stay on top in that respect, I could take advantage of her condition, but it's contrary to my personal code. If I took advantage of her, I'd live with it the rest of my life."

"I'm glad you told me that," said the doctor thoughtfully.

"Thanks. If I sounded sticky, I'm sorry."

Leibermann poured another drink. "You're among the favored because you have some appreciation for the principals of causality.

Wolff downed the last of his drink and shifted his cigarette to the opposite corner of his mouth. "So you think we'd better lower our sights and not try for the top of the mountain?"

"I think you should definitely do that and I think you know why. Will she be hard to convince?"

"No. She has been much smarter than I about that all along. She went along with the idea, hating every step of it. Actually, I think her main idea was directed at my ten percent. She appreciates what she calls my sensitivity in anticipating the little things where she's concerned. Money doesn't mean anything much to her. In prospect, I suppose, she'd admit to a desire to own pots of it, but she doesn't enjoy the pursuit of it." He nodded. "Yes, I'll kick the hell out of everything else but her writing and possibly an occasional lucrative TV offer."

"I think you should adjust her schedule so as to make it as easy as possible on her.

"Okay. I'll start thinking about it. I'm going to keep her here under lock and key for a good rest."

"I'm for that. Keep me informed." He got up, took a last look at the girl and went to the door. He faced Wolff and his eyes were wet with tears. "One word from you, you undersized leprechaun, and I'll bust you one."

Wolff grinned crookedly. "Okay, tough guy."

For three days, Marvelle stayed in the apartment, under sustaining sedation. She slept and ate and slept more. On the fourth day, she stopped medication on orders from Leibermann. On the morning of the fifth day, she looked at Wolff over her second cup of breakfast coffee. He was tired and drawn and she wondered if he weren't beginning to wear thin in his role of baby sitter. "Bern, this isn't being fair to you. I didn't realize what it could mean to you when I asked you to be a parent along with your other work."

"Shaddup," he told her inelegantly. "You're my baby and I'm going to keep watch over you."

"But you have other writers to look out for. You have your agency, your business."

"It was a chore until you came along," he assured her. "My partner can carry all those others. I'm not taking on anything until I have you lined out and sailing with the wind."

"That might turn out to be a very thankless, full time job."

"Let me decide whether taking ten percent from you isn't thanks enough ... along with you as a person. You're a pretty special sort, Marvelle.

She sighed. "This morning I woke for the first time in days with a clear sharp mind. I think my first waking thoughts were a drink and a man, in that order."

"That almost had to be," he said as though it were nothing. "Don't make it something it isn't."

"What's on for the day?" she said, anxious to change the subject.

He eyed her for a moment and put down his cup. "If you wanted it, you could have the world with a ring in its nose. You've had a three weeks taste of it. It got you because you weren't used to it. His eyes slitted. "Tell me about your acting past."

She thought for a moment. "I guess it goes back to when I was very young. I studied diligently how to make people notice me without becoming obvious ...

"The job," he said drily, "would have been to keep them from noticing you, and I think Conant's opinion was somewhat colored by the fact that you had him cross-eyed just watching you. Just the same that's his opinion and he has the test clip to prove it. When he speaks, others listen. All right. Like I say, you can do just about what you want. You're a phenomenon because you can be too many things too well. Movies will buy your novel just as sure as it's printed, and it'll be printed. I've read the rough draft...that of it you've written. It's got more aphrodesia by far than Lady Chatterly's Lover, which in my opinion has very little, but you have a flair for protective coloring that amazes me. The danger in your novel is that you make amorality sound so right and morally sound that it's hazardous."

She looked out over the rooftops of New York. "Until I started drinking, that was just the way I felt about it. An experience of the sense...the greatest experience of the senses. Something that made me feel whole and relaxed and enriched. When I started drinking and lost my sense of taste and fitness, then I began to hate myself."

"Let's not get sidetracked. Like I say, you have a fabulous career ahead of you. A career that any number of women I know would sell their souls to ten separate devils to equal. The rewards will be fame, money, position, adulation, admiration your name in lights...the works.

"Now...as I said before, many a woman would eat this up. Marvelle, I have serious doubts that you can take such a life, that you want it. I'll go along for the ride. I'll make you rich beyond your fondest dreams and myself along with you. I like money and I think you do, too, but I don't like it well enough to push you into this unless you want it with every atom of your being. That's a decision you'll have to make."

For a long time she was silent, toying with her coffee cup. Her robe had come open a little at the throat unnoticed and the plunging chasm between the smooth rising mounds of flesh was a reward to Wolff's all-seeing eyes. She looked up. "I've just thought of something. In all the rewards you mentioned, not once did you mention love."

He smiled sourly. "The omission was intentional. I'm afraid love of the sort you speak hasn't enough muscle and guts to fight its way through the jungle you'll be buried in...or succeeding in that, stay healthy once it succeeds. I've seen the mad efforts of people in the position you'll be in to find it. Some find it a dozen times...legally and a thousand times illegally. I've seen them wind up in a foam rubber room muzzled like mad dogs."

She gave him a steady calm gaze. "I don't want it, Bern."

Tears came to his eyes. "That's my girl," he said huskily.

"Now," she said crisply, "what's my alternative?"

"Write for your living and stay the hell out of the limelight...even New York. Have some privacy, maintain your own priceless identity, be the captain of your soul and give that love a chance to come into your life because believe me well, girl, the whole glittery game is a dead Christmas tree on New Year's Eve without it."

She leaped to her feet and slid into his lap, sinking her face into the curve of his neck "Bern, I wonder if I'll ever really be able to understand the fineness in you, to fully appreciate what a great person you are. You know better than I what you're giving up by giving me this kind of advice."

"All I'm giving up is money," he said stroking her soft shoulder. "I want you to be around for a long time because I want to be around you for a long time. You'll make plenty of money for both of us. Never fear."

CHAPTER THIRTEEN

Craine Frazer was in a steaming fury and at the moment grateful that no one had asked him why. He'd been instrumental in the discovery of the decade and the whole vast machine that was Crowder's was in a stir. Letters had poured in numbers never before recorded. There were the usual complaints and/or praise for some article or sort story, but the overall total gave ninety percent to the simple heartwarming story of "Marlene" by Marvelle Martingale.

The response was such that Sutton was excited, a phenomena in itself because he was known to be quite callous toward the efforts of authors, feeling that none of them could write a story deserving to be printed in Crowders, the only reason why they appeared was that the magazine could do no better.

"Well," said Miss Murdock coming into the office, "the joint is jumpin' and you look like you swallowed a fly."

Frazer looked up. "Don't heckle me, Gert. I feel like hell."

"Why?"

"I haven't been sleeping too well lately."

"I don't suppose it has anything to do with our new author."

He frowned at her then sat back in his chair. "How does a man make his sense of right and wrong come to terms with his..."

"Capacity to love someone?" she finished.

"Er... well, something like that."

"Longhorn, I'm afraid I won't be able to answer that for you. You know I realized something about like this would happen and

137

warned you that I wouldn't have her trodden upon. You make whatever compromise there is to make before you take the first step. I know what you must be thinking and I don't say you're a liar in what you saw. I just can't believe that you're putting the proper interpretation upon it. My instinct will not allow me to think the child is bad. We must remember in a case like this, that we're not in possession of *all* the evidence. Until we are, until we know everything there is to know, then we must defer judgment."

"And do what until all the evidence is in?"

Her eyes snapped. "Be forgiving... unless the word is unknown to you. Think back on some of your own shenanigans and try to conceive of what a scene there might have been if someone had turned on the light, peered through the transom. or rolled a potted plant out of the way electronically... with you as one of the principal actors. That shouldn't stretch your imagination too thin."

The color of his face attested to the accuracy of her stab.

She laughed. "See what I mean?" She took a seat and poured a cup of coffee from a thermos she carried. "This won't be Amanda's hairy-chested brand, but it'll pass. I did come in here with an idea." She handed the coffee to him.

"That's the first bright thing I've heard all morning. What is it?"

"I think you should see Marvelle every possible chance you get. You're an ass to sit back and be miserable on the strength of a bad case of love at first sight and disillusionment to wash it down with.

You haven't spoken two dozen words to her in your life. Anyone sending you a story as poorly plotted as your situation, wouldn't even get a decent rejection slip in his returned manuscript. You've got to get to know her, Longhorn. Maybe her qualities will outweigh her fragilities, but until you know something about them, that possibility won't help. Of course, you have no fragilities, so you may proceed positively shining with virtue."

He colored. "Look, you just came up with a terrific idea. Don't take away the shine by throwing bricks at it."

"I hear," said Miss Murdock lighting a cigarette, "she has offended the great grievously."

He grunted. "The great...whoever they are, should feel flattered. What great?"

"Hunt Harrington, et al. Bern took her up to see Bateman and Jones. Harrington is Bateman and Jones but the girls never know it until they are in too deeply to back out. That's when he pounces."

Frazer's eyes narrowed. "What do you know about him?"

"Plenty. You've just heard. I *know*...some of his victims, that is. Remember Vixen Mahler?"

"Yes...she was a house afire in pictures and TV for a while, then she dropped out."

"I've seen her. She hops bars now and sells herself to pay for her fixes. I have it straight that she's on heroin now and it won't be long."

"How do you know, and what's all that to do with Hunt Harrington?"

"She was his plaything for a few months. She lasted longer than most and had less guts. There've been several who started hitting the pipe when he chose them as companions. Others toughed it out until he was tired of them, gathered up what was left of their self-respect and went on. They were the tough ones. I know this because I knew Vixen Mahler when she was a child. I've know her mother for years."

"I've heard he was a poisonous sort."

"You just don't know. Believe me, when he's done with a girl, she's had it. There is no depravity under the sun that he hasn't practiced. Just as a sample, he cut Vixen's back up with a metal tipped belt until she was scarred for life, but they're the least of the scars she had."

"Why'n hell don't they leave him when it gets that rough?" He was pale and his lips set.

"A good many tried. The scarring came after Vixen tried to leave once. He sent a goon and brought her back."

"You mean in the middle of the most civilized city on earth that can go on?"

"Don't be naive, Longhorn. It can go on here easier than any other place. Think what would happen if he got his hands on Marvelle."

"What happened up there?"

"She threw a tizzy. The pace was too much for her, I suppose, and she chose that spot to throw a fit case of hysterics. As I heard it, Harrington didn't like it."

"You hear a lot."

"I sure do, and this I'd bet on. This you can bet on, too. He's never seen a girl like her. He'll want her as sure as shooting. If he wants her, he'll try to get her."

Frazer got to his feet. "Over my dead body."

"Mind if I steal that original observation for a story I'm writing?"

"Don't heckle me, Gert. You know Sam Mazzarelli."

"Sure, the retired cop. He writes."

"Yes, and we publish about six stories of his a year. I want to see him. Think you could locate him?"

"Sure. No strain. My boss keeps a file of addresses of writers and writes cheery letters to them from time to time and feels that he earns his money."

"Tell him to come in this afternoon if he can. If he can't, where can I meet him. The sooner the better." Frazer paced the floor, his imagination leaping ahead by leaps and bounds until has was as near frantic as he ever allowed himself to be. He got on the phone to Marvelle's apartment and Wolff answered. "You know about Harrington?" Frazer bit off.

"Sure, I know about him and I don't like any of it. Why?"

"Because the more I think about it, the more I'm certain he'll try to get his hooks on her."

Wolff was silent for a moment. "I'd thought about that but you hear so much about that guy..."

"Yeah, until you can't believe half of it. Just the same, you be on the lookout. I've got an idea coming up but it'll take a while."

"Marvelle's cooking up a Mexican lunch. Why don't you drop over."

"That's a better idea than some of your writers have. See you in twenty minutes."

Hunt Harrington was not idle either. His first impression of the girl hadn't been good. He had talked to Conant and heard the man foam with admiration, something Conant was not given to doing. He had sneaked and read her story and was appalled at the effect it had upon him Then there was the matter of Wolff who had called him things no man alive had ever called him. He'd take care of that, too, but it was a detail that could wait. Hunt Harrington didn't do his own dirty work. He hired it done and he knew almost to the minute where he could locate such men as he'd need for his widely varied misdeeds.

He walked into a very rich lounge on Fifty-First Street, scorned the bar and walked unobtrusively to a table in a dim corner and took a seat. To the casual onlooker he was a man looking for a pre-lunch martini. Tall, thin, narrow of shoulder, his green eyes glittering, his saturnine face set in hard repose. A waiter raised an eyebrow, but Harrington shook his head infinitesimally and cast his eyes to two severely well-dressed men seated at the bar. In thirty seconds they drifted casually to the table and sat down.

He let his eyes drift from one to the other and said, "Get her to my place."

They didn't reply... merely nodded. It was obvious that they had been briefed. They got up and left.

The waiter drifted over with a very dry martini. "Nice day, Mr. Harrington," he said conversationally.

Harrington nodded. "It'll be better."

"Yes sir." The waiter drifted away and Hunt Harrington sat for thirty minutes while he consumed the drink with great deliberation. Then he got up and left.

Wolff answered the doorbell without thinking it was other than Frazer who had made a fast trip and was not prepared to be pushed violently back into the living room.

"Who the hell are you?" he snarled alarmedly.

"A couple of guys," said the taller of the two. They were both funereally but well dressed, muscular and cold-eyed. The shorter one pulled a black leather object from his pocket and smashed Wolff callously on the side of his head. The little man crumpled to the carpet just as Marvelle, in shorts and apron, came from the kitchen, her hands held away from her as they were greasy from the meatballs she had been making.

"What do you want?" she said, her voice rising with each word. "What have you *done* to him?"

"Just a little tap, lady," said the short man. "He was getting ready to argue. We didn't come for argument. We came to get you. Now you be a good girl and get dressed in something real cool because our boss likes girls to dress cool. He's a hot rod himself."

"I don't know what you're talking about," she shrilled. "And I'm certainly not going anywhere."

The tall one reached out a long arm, caught her by the wrist and perked her to him so hard her shoulder felt pulled out of place. "Listen good, sister," he said harshly, "because I'm not going to tell you again. Get dressed. You're going with us. Either you go real quiet and without noise, or we'll fix you so your own parents won't know you. Harrington wants co-operation, but if he don't get it, he sure can be nasty. Now if you want to stay all pretty and happy, get your duds on because you're going with us or no man will be able to look you in the face again." He drew a switch blade knife, released her and with a swift sure motion slit her apron from breast to waist. "That's not your face, but it could have been."

She went sick and pale. Wolff was unconscious on the floor. These men were of a type she had never met before but she didn't doubt that they'd carry out their threat. The thought of the animal eyes of Harrington and her stomach went cold with dread. Never had she been so repelled by a man. Her shoulders drooping, she went through the door to her bedroom and closed it.

"Better see if she has a phone in there, Ed," said the shorter man.

The tall man nodded, went to the door and threw it open. He made a search and came out closing it. "No phone."

"Good. We just as well sit and take it easy. You in the bedroom, don't take all day."

They sat down and lit cigarettes, casting an occasional look at the unconscious form of Wolff.

Frazer, by the time he had driven to the Huntington Tower, was in a state. He'd been through the Korean Police Action and he had come out with a keen sense of caution, which when working saw an enemy in every man. He saw the two men walk into the Tower lobby some distance ahead of him and though he didn't know them, he filed them away in his mind. It took five minutes to park his car and when he got into the smoothly appointed lobby, they had disappeared. He almost went to the elevator but something stopped him and he went to the desk.

"Those two men who just came in," he said, "Where did they go!

"To Miss Martingale's apartment, sir."

"Did you ring her beforehand?"

"No sir. Mr. Wolff said it was all right to let people come up as long as he was there and there wasn't too many of them. When they come in droves, I let him talk to them first. There hasn't been many the last few days, so I didn't think it was necessary. Is anything wrong?"

"Probably not. Where are your phone booths?"

"Over there by the palms, sir."

He called Miss Murdock. "Did you get in touch with Mazzarelli?"

"He's on the other phone right now. He says he can meet you any place any time."

"Tell him to come to the Huntingdon Towers Apartment six twenty-two, and tell him to tie the throttle down."

"Trouble already, Longhorn?"

"Looks like it, Gert, Bye."

On the way up the elevator, Frazer, expecting the worst, wondered how he'd get in. He found the apartment number and pressed the button. "What is it?" asked a muffled voice from within.

"Registered letter for Miss Martingale."

There was silence, then he heard the girl's voice answering a low voiced conversation and he relaxed. She would open the door so he wouldn't be able to smash it open as he had intended had a man opened it.

She opened it and a glad cry burst from her lips as Frazer quickly stepped through. The men sprang to their feet, frowns creasing their foreheads.

"Cut, crum … this is a private party."

Frazer slammed the door, his eyes taking in the crumpled figure of Wolff on the floor. He was no longer the smooth suave editor of a big publishing house. He was a savage ready to kill. His blue eyes burned and a dull flush mounted to his cheeks. He catfooted forward and was met by the shorter man who slid his sap out and aimed well and hard. Frazer ducked under it, jack knifing his long body and slammed a whistling right into the midsection of the man who emitted his breath in a bleating whooshy cry. Hardly losing a step, Frazer slammed bodily into the taller man who was trying to get his knife out. He drove him backward, gripping the knife hand, twisting it with terrible power. The man's face went white as a particularly vicious twist seemed to tear the joints apart. The knife fell and a clubbed right fell on the side of his neck like a brick. He would have fallen but the furious Frazer now had him pinned back to the wall. He brought up a knee so hard that Frazer, catching it on his left thigh, felt the leg go dead. He swung the man away from the wall and bracing himself carefully, he sent a rocketing left to the man's jaw and dug a fearful right to the midsection ... and another left to the jaw. Frazer stepped back to let him fall and a scream sounded from Marvelle and a burst of lights exploded in Frazer's brain. He fell to one knee dazed but still fighting with enormous vitality to stay upright.

The short man had recovered and had used his sap. At about the same time, Bern Wolff also recovered. He had lain still for some time waiting until his faculties could be made to behave and when the man struck Frazer down, he came to his feet with the swift sureness of a cat. A lunge carried him to a table where a heavy bronze ashtray stood on curved feet made to resemble the feet of a bird. He swung the tray with all his might and it cracked suddenly on the skull of the short man. At this moment a tremendous man flanked by a younger, slimmer one, came through the doorway and shut it behind him.

"Real solid thump," said the giant as he went over and helped Frazer to his feet. "Your small friend here swings a mean ashtray. If that citizen ever gets up under his own power, I'll start playing the races."

Frazer shook the ringing out of his head and gripped hands with the big man. "I'd rather see you right now than a manuscript of yours. You got here just in time."

The big man laughed. "That's time enough. This is my boy, Craine. Johnny, meet Craine Frazer of Crowder's. He helped pay for your college." The slim, but well-knit man, shook Frazer's hand warmly. "Sure glad to meet you, sir."

Frazer said, "The man with the ashtray is Bern Wolff... oh, Marvelle, I'd almost forgotten you. Miss Martingale, Mr. Mazzarelli and another one not so big," They all shook hands, the younger Mazzarelli frankly charmed by the girl.

She smiled at them. "I was so scared I was frozen in a corner. No wonder Mr. Frazer forgot me."

"What's this all about?" asked the elder Mazzarelli.

Wolff rubbed the knot on his head. "Seems they wanted Marvelle," he began uncertainly.

"They're Hunt Harrington's boys," said Frazer metallically. "I'd like to hang him up by the ears."

"Not him," said Mazzarelli. "I was on the force for forty years. If it wasn't him we wanted, it was his father who was as bad. Hunt's real respectable. You'll never get anything out of those two."

"I'll take them in," said the younger Mazzarelli confidently. "That'll make my second day in plainclothes look good on the record book."

"This boy of yours a cop, too, Sam?" asked Frazer.

The big man smiled affectionately. "Sure. Tried to keep him off the force but he wouldn't listen. Now he's headed up faster than I went. He's got a degree, too, and that won't hurt."

He bent over the man Bern had struck. "We won't need the paddy wagon for this one," he said. "Better call homicide and let them tramp all over the place and do their job."

"What about me?" asked Wolff, seeming not particularly concerned, just asking for information.

"Well, one switch blade knife..." He felt around the dead man and found a gun. "One belly gun. Entering and attempted kidnapping." He grinned and straightened up. "'Solid citizen protects lovely young woman from abduction' makes a good headline, Mr. Wolff."

"All I have now is a head," said Wolff with a groan. "I'm not a bull-headed Brahma from the jungles of Texas who is hit harder than me and doesn't even get knocked out. I'm a highly tuned intelligent being whose head bone is thin as befits his intellectual capacities."

The house doctor was called for Wolff and Frazer, after satisfying the homicide squad, went off with the two Mazzarellis.

CHAPTER FOURTEEN

"Fill me in," said Sam Mazzarelli as they sat in a cool dim lounge over mugs of cold beer.

Frazer did so, not omitting the impact Marvelle had made on Crowder's, New York and now the country at large. The big man laughed.

"Hell, I know all that. I've been envying her. What's this with Harrington?"

"That had to do with a TV idea. Bern took her up to meet with the heads of Bateman and Jones, not knowing that the real head was Harrington. Marvelle flipped in their office but too many people know of Harrington's taste for good looking women and we were expecting something like this."

Johnny licked suds from his lips and said, "I don't think many have to be sent for. They're usually too willing to go."

"Yes," rumbled his father angrily, "and when they get a bellyful, that's when trouble starts. I wish I could prove half I know about him. He'd fry five times. What did you have on your mind calling on me, Craine?"

"I want a detective agency on the job. One that makes enough dough so Harrington couldn't buy them off."

"That's a tough order," said Johnny. "Money talks too loud."

"I have a better idea," said Sam, shifting his ponderous shoulders. "I'll take a shift, Johnny'll take one off duty or ask for leave, and we'll get a couple of more fellows that we can trust. People we know."

"If you'll do that," said Frazer gratefully, "you can write your own check."

The big man's eyes slitted. "Look, Craine, you don't own Crowder's. We don't aim to send a bill for a job we're doing a friend."

Frazer grinned. "You did that yourself.

"How did you get it?"

"My old man owns a hunk of Crowder's. I got to studying their setup and I thought I could improve on it. He got me the job, and I did what I thought I could do. It happens that everyone's happy over me. Crowder's, me and Pops."

"Well, dang me," said Mazzarelli using his worst oath. "I never knew that. So your old man owns half of Texas?"

"Not quite that much. Just a couple of hundred thousand acres and a few oil wells."

"And this editor business of yours ... just a play-thing?"

"In a way. I like it and I've stayed with it longer than I did with the drilling company, the real estate outfit or the breeding farm. I want to do a lot of things before I die."

"Now this Marvelle babe," put in Johnny, his dark eyes alight. "How long will this watch be?"

"Not long, I hope. Actually, I hope you two can find me some men and not have to do the job personally. Maybe oversee it."

"Want her covered all the time?"

"All the time." Frazer's heart seemed to turn over in his chest. Suppose she got drunk and went on the town ... "Another thing," he said through tight lips. "If she goes out to a bar and starts drinking, get her out of there and take her home. She's an alcoholic."

Frazer thought young Johnny would cry for a moment. "Now that's the awfullest thing I ever heard of," he said sadly. "What a hell of a shame."

"It's true and I hated to tell you, but I wanted you to know."

"What's your interest, Craine?" asked the big man raising an eyebrow.

"She's valuable property," he mumbled and feeling the older man's unbelieving stare, looked up. "All right. I'm soft on her."

"You were lucky today," said Johnny. "Man ... how lucky you were."

"Not entirely," said Frazer making rings in the table with his beer mug. Once suspicion is aroused, go on suspecting and the more you suspect the harder the work is, but the less likely you are to get into trouble."

Mazzarelli nodded heavily. "Suspect and back yourself up. Keep others knowing where you are."

"The minute I suspected Harrington," said Frazer, "I started suspecting everything and everybody. I called you and let you know where I was going. I saw those men going in ... not suspicious but I asked about them anyway. Found they were headed for her apartment. I told you to follow."

"Good police work as we all saw," said Mazzarelli looking meaningfully at his son. He turned to Frazer. "We'll set this thing up for you ..."

"And send me the bill," amended Frazer. "I hope it won't be for long."

Frank Miley was a rising young lawyer with more shrewdness than scruples and Hunt Harrington used him occasionally on matters requiring great discretion. He was seated in Harrington's office and the latter was saying, "It appears that Ed Scimica was a fool as was Jake Matta. They were recommended by you."

Miley squirmed. "It doesn't read right. I know everything that happened and too much happened against us for coincidence. I can't figure it. Frazer was not in the habit of visiting the girl and yet he went in not too far behind Matta and Scimica. Right behind him comes that retired Captain Mazzarelli and that youngster of his who is a sharp cookie by all accounts. Now why all the sudden descent on that apartment by so many?" He ran thin nervous fingers around his square chin. "I can't see that either of the men could have known all this would happen."

Harrington's green eyes were icy. "I don't pay for mistakes. You can tell that supposedly smart hood of yours, the one still alive, that he can swim or drown. Personally, if he drowns, it'll suit me fine."

"I'll tell him, Mr. Harrington."

"You do that. Now, have you any more dunces for hire... smarter than the others?"

The lawyer shook his head. "No man can foresee everything. If you want, I'll take care of it myself."

"You're no strong arm man, Miley. You're a good lawyer, but..."

"But I can plan it.

Harrington shrugged. "I'll have to admit that I spoke to them but, like you, I couldn't see who'd be suspicious because until I told them, the news was not out. I didn't speak half a dozen words to them. Get that girl here but if you goof it, don't come looking for me. I don't know you from a load of garbage. Now beat it."

For a long time Hunt Harrington sat and stared at the richly paneled wall. Never had any woman balked him for long and the memory of the girl writhing in Wolff's arms, the mouthwatering loveliness of her legs that were exposed halfway to the waist as she struggled, the straining of her breasts against the superbly fitted dress... all these things came back and sat like an acid poison on his stomach.

He had seen the revulsion that flickered like summer lightning through her nerves the instant their eyes met. He had known it for what it was and he hated her for it. He clenched his fists until the knuckles were white. He's have her. He'd strip her naked in his sound-proofed bedroom and he'd make her perform every degrading act his mind could devise. He'd pile humiliation upon humiliation upon her. Pain on pain. Insult on insult. He'd make her crawl and beg and he'd thrust upon her another task… and another and another, each more vile and hideous than the other.

The house doctor had convinced both Marvelle and Wolff that the latter should have x-rays made and undergo a general physical as the contusion was high on the temple, very close to the thinnest part of the skull. A sudden vomiting spell had been the clinching argument and now Marvelle sat in her apartment, alone for the first time in nearly four weeks. The door had hardly closed when she felt the tearing bite of desire for alcohol. Scarcely less was the demand of her loins, throbbing heavily with desire. For an hour she fought it valiantly and in the end she gave up as she had known she would Wolff had not replaced the whiskey he and Dr. Leibermann had drunk, but he had not reckoned with the shrewdness of an alcoholic. There were two bottles labeled sherry which she had brought along from the old apartment. She had filled them a long time back with hundred proof whiskey and kept them boldly in sight. She hadn't tried hiding them, but no one had seen or thought of her drinking sherry, so she provided herself with a four ounce drink of straight whiskey and though it gagged her, she held it down and finally after she caught her breath, chased it with a little ice water. Like a Madison Avenue sign she seemed to light up and glow with a heady soaring light. Her nerves and veins tingled and the demand of her flesh clamored louder.

Captain Samuel Mazzarelli, retired, nudged his son as the girl came through the revolving door of the Huntingdon Tower. "Anyone walking like that has some place to go. What if you went along and had to take her back to her apartment?"

Young Mazzarelli grinned. "Would that be bad?"

"And she tore her clothes off and gave you the unmistakable invitation… could you stay pure?"

The young man's face changed so fast it must have pained him. "No, sir," he answered instantly.

"In that case you, you stay here and watch the doorway for people who'd like to be there when she gets back. I'll go along with her. I'm the strong silent type."

"If I didn't know Mom so well, I'd give you an argument," said the young officer. "With her waiting back home, you'll be good, all right."

Marvelle had had three quick ones at the bar and her eyes were roving and as usual they didn't have to rove far. A slick lacquered article whose precise grooming looked contrived and not for hard rains or hot sweaty days sidled up. "Might I buy you a drink?"

She looked at him so hotly that he felt a little scared. "Of course ... although this seems like a dull place for a *tete-a-tete*."

He swallowed and goggled. He was accustomed to a more subtle acceptance and true to his devious kind, began to search the apple for a worm. He could find none, but was still wary. This babe was positive to the notch. but was still wary. Captain Mazzarelli interposed himself between him and the girl. "Run along, Buster," rumbled the giant. "You got things to do, I'm sure."

"Okay," said the man backing away hastily, bitterly. He had known it was too good to pan out. Dames like this always had a watchdog of some sort around either appointed or self-appointed.

She turned to the big man, her face cut in tired achy lines. "All right, sir, I'll go back quietly."

"That's my girl," he said heartily and helped her from the stool.

They walked by the cabstand where Johnny was in conversation with two taxi drivers. Big Sam nodded slightly as they passed and after an interval, Johnny followed them. They waited for him in the lobby of the Huntingdon Tower.

"Anyone come by?" asked the captain.

"Two. I wouldn't have paid them any attention except that one is a shyster used by Harrington, name of Miley. The other one has been arrested a dozen or so times but always managed to squeeze out and was never sentenced. They went up fifteen minutes ago."

"I wonder how they knew she left the apartment?"

"One of the cabbys knows her. They paid him fifty dollars to identify her as she came out."

The captain frowned. "Now that was a passing stupid thing to do. Why do you suppose he did it?"

"Cabbys keep a pretty closed mouth as a usual thing. I suppose Miley's just smart enough not to get run over, but outside the lawbooks, he's no genius."

"Let's go on up." Marvelle's drinks had begun to die out and she was beginning to tremble and shake. Her high-spiked breasts were hypersensitive and the tips were cherry tipped thorns digging at the material of her bra. She glanced sidelong at Johnny Mazzarelli and began to plot how she could get him alone. The older man, she thought, might be proof against her charm but she had felt the younger man's eyes on her earlier and she knew he didn't have a chance. Furious throbs of naked voluptuous sensation washed her like tidal waves and she pressed her knuckles to her forehead ... leaning against the side of the elevator.

"I want this man's hide," said Sam as they got out of the elevator. "Kid, do you have the nerve to go in alone so we can stay back and listen?"

She thought of Hunt Harrington and nodded. "I'll do it."

"Good girl. We won't be ten steps away."

She took out her key, turned the lock and stepped in. She closed the door almost shut but left an inch.

When she turned, she gasped as she saw the men. "What do you want?" she flared.

Miley made his approach suavely. "Mr. Harrington would like to see you. He's prepared to make you a star. You'll make more money than you ever dreamed of before. He sent me to say he'd like you to come to his office."

"What's the other man for?"

Miley laughed. "Oh, that's just Pepper Lemmon. He's a friend of mine. He'd seen your picture and wanted to see if you were real."

"I'm not going anywhere and you can tell Mr. Harrington for me that I'll see him in hell before I'll come to his office and I don't need his filthy money. He tried to have me kidnapped already today. I think he's pushing his luck."

Miley's attitude changed. "Okay, sister. I was giving you the easy way. If you make us, we can do it the hard way."

"You'll never get me down from here."

"That's what you think, Peter, show her the pill."

The slim blonde man with a sharp face and nose didn't speak but dug in his pocket and pulled out a small box and extracted a single white tablet.

Miley took the pill between two fingers. "I can either ask you to take this or make you take it. When you're asleep we'll call an ambulance. You'll merely be a sick girl..." He sniffed in her direction. "Or a drunk one. It'll be very simple."

"Except for one thing," said Captain Mazzarelli as he stepped through the door followed by his son.

Lemmon looked like he was about to run and Miley went so white that his face was ghastly.

Johnny's hand lashed out like a striking snake and plucked the pill from Miley's palsied fingers. He took the box from Lemmon and dropped it in. "This will look good in court as well as what we heard," he said happily.

"And if you manage to weasel out of that," said the father, "the Bar Association will no doubt be interested since I know they've been interested in you before. Slap the jewelry on them, Johnny."

When they had gone, Marvelle began to pace up and down like a caged tigress. She took a long fierce drink from the bottle with the sherry label and began to pace again.

She whimpered and squeezed her face between her hands until she could see a horde of golden lights passing in review. Through the dense fog of approaching panic, a thread of sanity told her that unless someone stopped her, she'd do several things. She'd continue drinking until a point was reached, then she'd go looking for a man. In prospect she could envision the next morning, either here looking at her own ceiling and suffering tortures of the damned for what she had done, or worse still in a strange apartment, looking at a strange ceiling and maybe with one or several strange bedfellows. She stopped pacing, sat on the couch and stared hard at the wall. If she could foresee the future with such clarity, why couldn't she do something to avoid it? She thought of calling Wolff but she remembered that he was at the hospital undergoing a physical examination. She thought of Frazer and her soul curdled against this move. She wouldn't be able to stand his quiet, thoughtful eyes, knowing they had seen her in the most despicable act she had ever performed. Her mind, quickly to the defensive, rephrased it. The most despicable act she had ever allowed to be performed upon her. She took a deep breath. There was no use trying to make it better by the rephrasing of a thought. She and Larsen had performed worse, times on end. But was it worse... or even bad? Again came the defensive thought. With Larsen it hadn't seemed bad and now she arrived at the point that had eluded her before. Being exposed to all these people and Frazer. That had been the terrible thing. Not the act itself. Strangely she felt better. Maybe someday he'd understand that part of what had happened. He'd admitted that even though he had seen and had been revolted, he still thought highly of her. She crumpled to the couch and wept harsh bitter tears. Oh God, why had it been *him* that saw her. Why not ten million others? Why Craine Frazer? A shocking thought startled her into sitting position. Why was she thinking these thoughts. Why had she singled Frazer out of all the men she had known as the one she most wanted to revere and respect her? The full realization burst upon her and sent her cowering in a pitiful huddle on the couch, dry eyed now, but aware of a desperate misery so acute that she knew she would not be able to stand it for long. *She was in love with him.* For the first time, Marvelle Martingale, a girl dedicated to the rites of Aphrodite since an early age, was faced with the grand passion for the first time in her life. The misery was the results of the belief that he considered her dirt and probably wouldn't want to even be seen with her.

Out of sheer desperation, she got up and called Crowder's and asked for Miss Murdock.

"What is it, my dear?" asked the older woman urgently, shocked at the girl's voice.

"They...sent Bern to the...hospital...I'm alone. Miss Murdock...please send someone to put me away and keep me put away until I...can get a grip on myself. I'm going stark staring mad sitting here alone...I just can't stand it anymore. I'm bitterly sorry to always be causing people trouble but..."

"Shut up," barked Miss Murdock. "Are you drinking?" "Y-y-yes. I've been drinking."

"Now I want you to do exactly as I tell you. Go pour yourself a big one and sit on your couch and drink it slowly. I'll be there as soon as a taxi can get me there. Do you understand?"

"Yes...and thank you, Miss Murdock. Believe me, I wouldn't be bothering you but I just don't have anyone else to call on, and...please hurry."

"You do just as I told you."

Miss Murdock walked into Craine Frazer's office. He was dictating a letter to the overblown Miss Allen.

Miss Murdock gave her a scorching look. "You can leave us, Allen. This won't take long."

Miss Allen compressed her lips but the look in the older woman's eyes made her close her notebook and leave the office.

Miss Murdock faced him squarely. "Longhorn, who's with Marvelle right now?"

"No one. I just had a phone call from Sam. He and Johnny got two more. Got that shyster he's wanted for so long. She's alone now. Why do you ask?"

"She's just called. All this has the girl at the end of her tether. If someone doesn't go around there right now she might just take a long dive from her window. I never heard her in a state like she is now."

"Damn," he muttered. "You going around there?"

"No, you are."

"*Me.*" He squeaked a little. "Why me?"

"Because I think it's time you meant something to her. You're in love with her and the sooner you get the snakes, slugs and assorted trash out of your brain and admit it, the sooner she'll become a normal human being again. You've sat around the edges and suffered. I think it's time you did a little suffering in the middle of things. I'm telling you, she's desperate. You'd better act fast."

He acted fast against the impulse to proceed with caution, because he was, in his own way, as confused as Marvelle. He did have the presence of mind to call Dr. Leibermann and ask him to meet him at the apartment He realized as soon as he had done so that it was an act of cowardice. He was afraid to see her alone.

CHAPTER FIFTEEN

He met Dr. Leibermann in the lobby but he was fated to see her alone after all.

"Mr. Frazer," said the doctor after he had listened to the explanation, "this is one time when though I may be needed, I don't think I should appear. It has become a sort of rote for me to make an appearance, give her a sedative, then blow. All that is pure stop-gap operation. We're no closer to her trouble than before. Now. it Is my opinion that she should have rest, observation, congenial company and an occasional skull session with me. It will take time and having me pop in and out like a jack-in-the-box will establish a sort of habitual thing that I'm trying to avoid. I do not care for analysis for that very reason. Too much dependence eventually rests with the practitioner and he becomes a drug and the patient becomes an addict. I don't care for those methods. I don't practice them. Certain isolated cases, where the indication is clearly drawn, I use analysis as a *part* of the regimen. I do not see it as the complete thing. Now I suggest that you go on up. If, when you've seen her, you still feel that she needs a doctor, then I'll come up. I'll wait for you in the lobby."

Frazer, his chest a boil of confusion, started for the elevator, then stopped and came back. "I'd like to have a session with you myself."

Dr. Leibermann smiled. "Mr. Wolff told me about you. I think you'll be good for the girl but I warn you, she is in a state now where it is very easy for her to form a strong attachment for anyone who represents a stout shoulder and a refuge. You must remember this."

"That's exactly what I want to talk about. I'll call you for an appointment."

Frazer knocked and heard the swift patter of feet as she raced to open the door.

She threw it open and gasped with disappointment, a deeply hidden joy, and a fear that was not so deeply hidden. He could see a picture of tumultuous racing of opposing impulses that passed through her mind plainly printed on her face. She gulped.

"I … I … was expecting Miss Murdock."

He grinned crookedly. "I'm sorry to disappoint you."

She shook her head. "No … it isn't that at all. I'm … I'm … just," a quick rigor shook her. "I don't know why you came, Mr. Frazer. I'm nothing to you. I couldn't be anything to you."

"Let's don't say that. I came because Miss Murdock said you were in a state."

She ran fingers through her hair and spun around, her breath coming in gulps. "I'm in a state … I have no one to turn to. Bern's in the hospital." She turned to him her enormous eyes wide with despair. She dragged her fingernails cruelly downward across her cheeks. "I want to be put away before I lose my mind. I'm at the end. I don't know what to do …"

All of a sudden she went into a hard convulsion and would have fallen but he caught her and took her to the couch where he held her close, like a small child until the spasm ended in a fit of frenzied weeping. Then she clung to him after the first intensity had worn itself out and wept quietly until finally she went to sleep, her wet face clinging to the curve of his neck, her arms tight about him. When she had sunk deep enough into sleep that her arms relaxed, he gradually, and with much care, deposited her on the couch and arranged her clothing that had become disheveled. Even in her sleep, she'd draw a shuddering sobbing breath that would calm the instant he touched her forehead with a gentle hand. His heart ached fiercely and the thickness in his throat threatened to suffocate him. She moaned faintly in her sleep and her body moved in a slight sinuous wave that made his breath catch in his throat. Even in her sleep it seemed every move she made was that of a finished voluptuary. He examined her with care. Certainly she must be made of excellent materials because dissipation had not produced a single wrinkle and her skin was as alabaster pure as when he had first seen her. Her body was still a poem in curved perfection, her breasts still valiant in their eager pout.

He went to the phone and called the lobby. Dr. Leibermann was still there.

"I don't think I'll need you," said Frazer in a guarded voice.

"What happened?"

"Well, she went into a sort of convulsive panic when I first got here, but I sort of cuddled her a while and she quieted then fell into a deep sleep."

"Now, Frazer, I want to tell you exactly what happened. You caught her at a bad moment and you provided something she sorely needed. You became at once a protector and a defender. Your actions quieted her fears either real or imagined. You became someone to whom she could cling. You now represent a haven. Wolff would have done just as well but I must point out that the girl has considerable regard for you, which is not the same thing she feels for Wolff. He represented a person, a very nice sympathetic person, but no more. I feel that you will represent something a lot more profound. I think you should start thinking about that very seriously. I needn't outline what it will mean to her to achieve a really deep abiding attachment to you, then find herself denied. Do you follow me?"

"I follow you," said Frazer dully. "I'd just as soon not comment at the moment. My own mind is trying to turn traitor."

"Better have that appointment with me as soon as you can."

"I'll do that, but I don't think she should be left alone until either Bern or Miss Murdock can be in attendance."

"That is a very wise reaction. People like Miss Martingale shouldn't be left alone. It is their peculiarity that aloneness is a play of horrors that descend upon them whenever they're forced to be by themselves. Note one thing, however, being alone presented no problem until she started drinking."

"All right. I'll call you as soon as I get relieved."

"Do that."

Frazer hung up the phone carefully and turned back to the girl. His misery and tension increased until he felt that every nerve was pumping. He went into the kitchen to look for whiskey but could find none. Tentatively he picked up a bottle of sherry. but he was in dire need of a drink and he didn't know how long his vigil might last. He tilted the bottle, intending to take a gigantic slug of wine and was almost garroted by the savage bite of hundred proof whiskey. Frantically he drew a glass of water and gulped it, trying to catch his breath at the same time. After a time he felt his assaulted esophagus retreat from seared anger and he had to chuckle at himself. He turned and looked at the gracefully sprawled figure of the girl. So this was another facet of an alcoholic. Someone might throw away her whiskey but no one would think of throwing away cooking sherry. He made himself a highball and almost gagged. His throat and stomach were not yet mollified from the initial assault and he had to drink more plain water. A slight ringing in his head suggested that he had taken a ferocious jolt of straight whiskey before he could stop and on his empty stomach it was reacting already.

Frazer probably knew but had probably forgotten that there is a point which, if reached suddenly in drinking, is a good starter and he had reached it. He had consumed three strong highballs by the time she was awake and everything seemed sunny and bright. He had produced some upsetting inner stirrings just watching her writhe sleepily and come awake. When she sat up and smiled at him, he felt slightly wounded.

"Did I go to sleep on you?"

He sat beside her and pulled her into an embrace. With a sigh she relaxed against him and pillowed her head on his chest. "Thanks for being so decent about everything," she said softly.

Blood seemed congealed in a choking clot in his throat. He wanted to speak but he was afraid his voice would not behave.

"Being decent?" he managed to get out. "Do I deserve thanks for merely being decent?"

She stirred in his arms, then sighed contentedly.' 'Well, you were decent to come here when I needed someone. To leave your office and drop everything just because I was about to blow away like dry leaves. Especially when I know what you must think of me."

"I wish you wouldn't bring that up," he said shortly. "Somehow that seems far off...a long time ago."

She shuddered. "Maybe so, but I'll never forget it."

She raised her head and studied his face exactingly. "You're just like I first pictured you even though I was drunk. You've a good face. I feel like it will always be the same. It will get older but it will never change." She smiled. "You've been drinking."

He nodded and the pain of her overpowering attraction was shaking him sorely. Without being able to stop himself be bent his head and kissed her gently on the lips. She stirred and went bonelessly quiescent in his arms. Her lips parted for the entry of a sweetness that almost made her faint. His kiss was no longer gentle but still soft and thrumming with a love that nothing could withstand. Then it grew more insistent as passion began to lash his bloodstream into thundering activity. She swung her head from side to side in an agony, a strangling sob tearing its way from her depths because she could see what it could be like and yet she felt it could never be hers. That she knew she would never be able to stand.

Frazer was never sure what the drinks had to do with the fact that he lost all balance, lost his usually keen awareness, lost the restraint that had been born a part of him and slipped into her toils almost without a single thought that danger might be lurking. The fragrant softness of her, the supple animal that emerged as usual with a single primordial goal and sought it with a heat and passion that was a part for Frazer's complete capitulation.

Her breasts came under his attention and for a split second he stared at them with stony fixity then their pristine purity and divinity of sculpture. trembling and reaching eagerly for him broke the spell and he kissed them with hot avidity, careful however not to bruise their tender summits. Gradually as her clothes disappeared, she emerged from them like a rose being born in a dew drenched mist and she shone pinkly through it as though touched by the first virginal ray of a new sun. Suddenly, madness deserted her and though the heat of passion still blasted her, she was keenly aware of everything that went on. Instead of the insane strength of fevered search, there was a stunned, almost anesthetic lassitude that now pervaded her, and she wept and whimpered from it as though the ordeal was becoming too much for her to bear. She realized tardily that this was something totally new, something vastly different from anything that had ever happened to her. He was taking her place and he was the one who was losing perspective, he who was stripped of his thin veneer of civilization. She arched her nude body toward this new and fabulous wonder, felt the exciting touch of his bare skin, felt his breach the defenses that were not defenses at all. Then the weakness left her and she felt light and stimulated, receiving the wonder that was him with a deep fundamental cry of unendurable ecstasy and in return gave him a similar wonder that was her. His embrace was crushing and her acquiescence was absolute. She was his utterly, completely, with a sense of all giving and all receiving, such as she had never known. She stepped across the threshold that divides the madness of mere passion and that sacred chamber of the union of true great love.

For a long time they lay still, their ears deafened by the echoes of that mightiest of all music but as is the way with women, her heart was overflowed with a tenderness that knows no rest. She kissed his face and hair, she stroked his head and murmured an endless incoherent verse of love, caressing his body subtly. Her breasts were taut and sharp against his chest.

At long last he stirred and sat up shaken ... so terribly shaken that he had to fight valiantly for thought. He drew a hard harsh hand over his face while Marvelle sat up, drawing her legs beneath her, examining the devastation she had wrought, wondering what went on in his mind, wondering if she had lost him for all time. She crawled to him and clung to his left arm. "I'm so sorry, Mr. Frazer ... so bitterly sorry that every memory of me should be ..." She started to cry, massaging her forehead against his arm in an agony of humiliation. She crawled into his lap and forced herself against the shaggy pelt of his chest, begging piteously, incoherently ... and she herself was not quite sure what it was she begged for.

Marvelle slipped to the floor to her knees and rested her head against his knees, hugged her breasts with her arms and wept scalding tears that coursed down his legs. Craine Frazer came back to the present by slow painful degrees. The shock of her humiliation was such that he went weak with revolt. She had given him the most precious possession she had and had made a moment in his life that he would not forget and yet she was begging his forgiveness. With a tremendous effort, he refrained from some violent protest. Calmly he caught her face in his hands and lifted it.

"Marvelle ... what on earth are you talking about?"

She fought hard to smile through the misery and tears, but was a trembly travesty that felt like a knife in his chest.

"If...you don't know...maybe it doesn't...matter..." She climbed into his lap again and wept as though her heart would break. He held her close and crooned softly to her, stroking the velvety surface of her shoulders, caressing and soft masses of her hair.

With complete consciousness came memory and it flowed through his veins in an icy flood. Gently he placed her on the couch and got up. He put on his clothes and turned to face her. She hadn't made any attempt to dress but sat huddled, her long lashes stuck together with tears, looking at him half fearfully ... as though his next words might be her life sentence.

"I'm going to have to leave for a while, Marvelle. When I come back, I hope to have a lot to say. Are you afraid to stay by yourself if I leave?"

She shook her head slowly. "I feel right now as though I'll never be afraid again."

He bent and kissed her. "I'll come back as soon as I can. Meantime maybe Bern will come in."

Before he could tie his tie, Bern knocked at the door. Marvelle ran to the bedroom to dress and Frazer opened the door.

Wolff came in, his hands jammed hard in his jacket pockets. He looked at Frazer who turned red.

"I saw a man run over once by an M-4 tank who looked better than you," he rasped slowly.

Frazer was acutely uncomfortable. "Can you stay with her? I've got some place to go."

"You remind me of a little boy who, having some place to go and being short of time, had already gone."

Frazer flushed scarlet again. "Dammit, will you stay?" he yelled.

"Sure. That's why I came back. My head is all right."

"That's open to question," snapped Frazer, feeling pleased that he had been able to make even a weak retort.

Wolff grinned. "Well, you're coming back to normal anyway. Be on your way. Where's the queen?"

"In the bedroom getting dressed..." Frazer paused in heart-stopping panic and Wolff chuckled drily.

"Man, why don't you go while you're still able? You're positively apoplectic."

"I could murder you," growled Frazer as he walked rapidly from the apartment, slamming the door behind him. His neck, when last seen, was still turkey red.

"You people," said Dr. Leibermann with a smile, "have ruined my office routine. Luckily, I had an appointment that I could drop to a later hour. Ever since the marvelous Marvelle came into my life. I'm never sure if I'll get through a day without having to get my nurse to get on the phone and lie for me. You look as though a runaway horse had dragged you some distance."

Frazer groaned. "You and Wolff. At least you have professional standing and I can tell you." He told the doctor everything and when he was through, his face was drawn and somewhat pale. "I never knew it could do that to you. I've still got that worm back in my head. I don't think it could stop me now but I want to get it out of there before I do anything positive about her."

"If I can make you admit that there is no worm in your head," asked the doctor, "what then would your reaction be?"

"I'm not sure I follow you."

"Did you ever hear of narcosynthesis?"

"I've heard of it. Not much, but the term is familiar."

"I gain control over your conscious mind by wetting it down and out of the way by a drug. When the proper state is reached, you will answer questions which I will not be able to push conscious obstacles in the way of truth. Now I have some news for you. Moral dudgeon is not an inherited thing. You have a capacity for it, but morals per se are acquired ... to whatever capacity you may, as an individual, have. Too many things are done for apparently moral reasons when in truth there were no moral factors involved at all. A great mass of people are as moral as they can be because they think if they're not, they won't get to heaven.

Others are moral because it gets them applause from a certain social strata or maybe individuals. There are people, of course, who are convinced that a moral life is the only way to live. I'm not speaking of these. What I propose to show you is that the moral trauma you suffered from the breach of good taste or whatever you want to call it, is not a part of the inner workings of one Craine Frazer. I'm going to make you a tape recording of your answers, most of which you will remember. I'll present you with the tape anyway for a wedding present."

Frazer laced his slim fingers together. "Let me see if I get you right. What you're saying is that with the same removal of inhibition, I might perform about as she would?"

"The comparison is rough but not too amiss. You see, there are individual degrees of the relaxation of the inhibitory reflex just as there is in any other reflex. Let me pose you a simple example. Four stout drinks might make you feel a delightful tingle. Give Marvelle the same four drinks and she's ready for a man. Her threshold is lower than yours, but we must remember that invoking the shades of psychic determinism, no two people have the same threshold. Pain is another example. Personally pain makes me get gray and vomit. I've seen some stoics sit still with a crushed foot and never turn a hair. Individual threshold again plus another factor not so easily explained and it is what we call guts. Some have it and some don't. A person with a low pain threshold and guts will stand it. Another with a higher threshold and less guts can't. So, it is my opinion that if one could remove in you the exact degree of inhibitory reflex as Miss Martingale experienced on that fateful night, give or take a little, you'd perform no better than did she. You see, Mr. Frazer, what we must remember is that conscious, iterate, progressive and fruitful thought and awareness is the only way man, the animal, differs from his lower order brethren. We've progressed to a higher plane of mental activity and of course we have the prehensile hand which is a help. Just the same, take away in some manner this levelling catalyst that keeps us socially acceptable, and we're back to our animistic habits. Sometimes we act worse than the animals because we carry with us, back to this jungle frame of mind, some of the dishonesties we learned and that makes us a fearsome animal indeed." Dr. Leibermann smiled. "As you've probably deduced, I like to hear myself talk."

Frazer eyed him calmly. "I like to hear you talk, too. You make some remarkable good sense, the sort you feel embarrassed that you didn't think of yourself. Let's get on with it."

"Very well." He depressed the key to his intercom. "Miss Steiner, will you bring in the infusion set … Sodium Amytal. Yes. Immediately."

"You're a jerk," said Wolff dispassionately, his mouth twisted acridly.

Marvelle pitched her exquisite eyebrows. She grinned at him like a pixie. "I ain't neither."

"Spare me your mid-west argot. I say you're a jerk, a pill."

"Why, because I'm so in love with Mr. Frazer that I can't half think or see?"

"Yes," he growled. "Love is a playtoy for children. Love is a sick man's dream of some puffy paradise where people eat lotuses and drink such swill as nectar."

"You're a hard man, Mr. Wolff."

"Shut up. You irk the tail off me and you know why?"

"No, why?"

"Because I envy you so that it hurts me all over."

She came and sat beside him and touched his cheek with a soft palm. "No matter what, Bern, I'll always love you. Knowing you has been one of the greatest things that ever happened to me."

His eyes became moist, a film that almost obscured the cynicism. "I'm going to clip you one in the teeth if you don't shut up. Hell, have a drink."

She started. "That's funny, I hadn't even thought of a drink."

"Now that you've thought of it, do you want one?"

"Yes," she said miserably, her mouth losing its gaiety. "But I can't. Mr. Frazer might come back."

"Well, that listens like progress. No more advances from the subtle Mr. Harrington?"

"No …" she shuddered. "Bern, that man scares me to death."

"You're well advised to be scared of him, but he hasn't given up. He's lost a couple of rounds and losing is a strange state to him."

CHAPTER SIXTEEN

Mr. Hunt Harrington had succeeded for so many years that defeat to him was unthinkable and yet he was forced to think of it. A chit of a girl and some jerk literary agent. He had made several mistakes. His first one had been the sending of two untried hoods to bring her back. A number of things had happened to that deal that no one could have foreseen. Then that fool of a lawyer had tried to turn good ... much too soon after the other defeat and now both he and his friend languished in jail. He chuckled savagely. At least there was some gratification in that. Hunt Harrington could correct the mistakes he had made. The torture he was suffering now could not long endure, so something had to be done soon. He was half drunk on martinis, something that hadn't happened to him in twenty years. He had learned that a clear mind was indispensable in his business. He did not know that his mind was at the moment not quite clear. It seemed to be as sharp as a razor and as pellucid as spring water. This was a delusion and a snare and Hunt Harrington fell into it. An almost psychopathic egoist, he strutted before his mirror and admired the many things that made him a handsome irresistible man. No other women had been able to resist him. Of course, some needed a little coaxing of the proper sort, but they always capitulated. Harrington's mind was in such a state, what with the position he had occupied for years and the martinis he had consumed, that it was quite incapable of registering the truth which was that women were invariably terrified of him and did his bidding only under tremendous pressure or tremendous ambition.

He had not been denied for so many years that it was very easy for him to treat his successes as due reward for his personal magnetism. He straightened. That was it. See her himself. Make quite a program of apology... He stopped. He had never apologized to anyone in his life. He paced up and down until sweat started out on his forehead. What was an apology that was not meant? Tactics, just tactics. What did it matter if his mouth apologized? He would visit her. He would apologize for the clumsiness of his minions. He would offer to make restitution. He would offer her a career so glittering that, being a woman, she could not possibly turn it down. He took another martini. The business was settled and the annoying tension was less. He smiled grimly. She'd suffer that apology. She would suffer like no one had ever suffered since time began... and Hunt Harrington drifted closer to the edge of a void that he had been approaching for years.

"Since I didn't get to serve the Mexican dinner the other day," Marvelle was saying, "I'll defrost it and serve it to you tonight. Do you think Mr. Frazer will come back?"

Wolff fixed his eyes on her. "If what I think happened, nothing short of a tidal wave putting twenty feet of salt water on Broadway could keep him away."

Her eyes softened. "Bern, I don't even have half an impulse to lie to you. Does that make me bad?"

He dragged fiercely at a cigarette and emitted a dense cloud of smoke. "I'm beginning to wonder if you don't have about you something that makes pretty much anything you do right. One thing sure. No one can hold it against you very long. As far as I'm concerned, you're still a small-town little girl who tried to swim before you learned to wade. You shipped a little water aboard and it began rattling around in your bilge and frightened you. No one with your early conception of the depths and heights of emotional clamerings can be all bad."

"And yet it was an emotional involvement that sent me off the deep end."

"That is a peculiarity that demands examination. It seems that your knowledge of emotions was innate and did not spring from experience. No one ever has enough happen to them to write wholly from experience. I think the delight of your writings in one sense is that you know emotions and yet you treat them with a delicate detachment that is almost never done. In other words, you dealt very deftly with emotion without having any of your own to take over and personalize the sequence therefore taking it out of the experience of a good many readers. That's why you reach so many people where a more personalized writer would fail...answer the phone."

She picked it up, answered and went white. "Yes...I'm Miss Martingale...Just a moment, I'm undressed." She clamped a hand over the mouthpiece. "It's *him*."

"You sure?"

"Positive."

"Then play along with him. Pretend interest. If he wants to come up, tell him you're alone."

She tried to speak but the hell boiling in Wolff's sunken eyes numbed her tongue for a few seconds.

"All rightie," she said in forced good humor. "I'm decent now. What did you want...I mean who are you?" She sat down and took courage by pure will power. "Oh, Mr. Harrington...well, your attentions haven't been of the kindest, if you know what I mean. Yes, I'm alone. Why?"

She narrowed her eyes at Wolff and nodded. "Why, I think that would be nice. Tomorrow night...at what time? Eight will be fine. I'm really sorry I threw a fit in your office. I was all unstrung and frightened to death...Fine. Tomorrow night at eight. 'Bye." She cradled the instrument and Wolff caught her by the shoulders.

"Steady, kid. You won't be alone tomorrow night. That I promise."

She clutched him and steadied herself. "Or Bern...I almost couldn't do it. His voice just made me cold all over, like a snake crawling down my back."

"Now listen to me," he said shortly. "Tomorrow night at eight there must be just you and me. If Frazer wants a date, make it at ten or some other day. No one here but you and me."

She nodded. "Just you and me, Bern...Bern, what's going to happen?"

"I can't tell you. Just play it my way, kid and you won't have a thing to worry about."

In the back of his mind, Wolff was toying with an idea that might easily mean his death. If this eventuality crossed his mind, it didn't penetrate the saturnine granite of his features. He remembered something he had heard about Hunt Harrington a long time ago. He was a coward and never went out without a weapon under his arm. His clothes were specially tailored to prevent the bulge from being apparent.

Aside from a feeling of delicious lassitude, Frazer felt no effects from his recent ordeal and it had been an ordeal. He recalled confessing things led on by the probing questions of Dr. Leibermann that fairly made his flesh crawl. He fidgeted and wriggled uncomfortably. "I don't think we need play the tape back," he said sweating with embarrassment.

"Oh yes, we do," retorted the doctor. "I'll leave if you don't want a witness, but after all, I heard the original so it would be a little silly. Do you know why I want to be present?"

"Er...No, I don't suppose I do."

"Because you have a normal compliment of the human drive to duck something that seems unpleasant. Right now you're wriggling because you remember most, if not all, you said. I want you to listen to yourself talk. I want us both to listen...we're both perfectly conscious, remember. You said it. Now I want you to listen to what you said."

"Did I mean it?" asked Frazer a trifle timidly.

"If you didn't, then your entire unconscious is a pile driven liar."

"Okay. Run it."

He sat and listened and sweated and squirmed through the entire playback, listening to a male animal tell in concise understandable language just what he'd do, given opportunity, provocation and complete freedom of action, No, none of these things nauseated him in prospect. Yes, he understood that they were not in the least abnormal. Yes, he understood that the act of shying away from it came not from inner revolution but from the attitudes of society, from the fear of what the partner might think or say or do. Yes he understood the definitive difference between perversion and diversion. Yes, he might have used the former term when the latter really applied.

When it was over, Dr. Leibermann stood up. "Frazer, you've cooperated and that's to the good. I've reached into your mind to a depth you could not have achieved without my methods. You have had a conscious look at the cellar. You now know what *is* without all the moral conventional and social trappings. Now, what you do about it is another thing entirely. I always take the attitude that most of my patients are essentially sound in the crumpet. Once they've seen a fact then the next step is to admit it. After that comes acceptance of it with all the attendant vapors and sweat. It's the really hard thing to do." He shrugged expressively and gestured toward the tape. "We've hung your soul out to dry there. Take it with you and whenever you are tempted to slip back in your old way of thinking, run it and listen hard." He grinned. "I don't know whether you have the guts, but why don't you play this tape to Marvelle? That, in a sense, would put you on an equal footing with her. She wouldn't have to depend on any heavy declaration from you to prove any point you might want to make regarding this affair."

Frazer mopped his cold damp face and got up. "Give me those things and let me get out of here. I've got some thinking to do."

He called Marvelle, found that Wolff was in attendance, made a fearfully lame excuse for not paying her a visit and went to his apartment.

"Boy, you look wrung out," declared Amanda with a penetration that didn't improve Frazer's state of mind. "I got leg of lamb for dinner."

"Make me a light sandwich," he said numbly. "I'm going to get steaming drunk."

"What for?"

"Because I need to think."

"I ain't never been in the knowledge that drinkin' was good for thinkin'."

"Have you ever been drunk, Amanda?"

She erupted in laughter. "Look, boy, back when I was young, I was a *thaing.* Me'n Rooster used to get drunk every Saturday night and fight plumb till the next Monday".

"Well, do you remember how your thoughts used to run around when you were drunk?"

"I sure do, but I don't remember 'em ever gettin' me any place."

"I want to let mine loose, let 'em run around and take a good look while they're running."

"All right. I'll stand by and see you don't go hurt yourself."

"Thanks," he said sarcastically and she bridled instantly.

"Don't you go gettin' brassy with me, boy, or I'll tan your breeches. If you all screwed up in the head, then it's about that pretty little girl you brought here that time, and as far as she's concerned, there ain't but two ways for you to go. Either you dig back in your head and forget what she done or you can just kiss her goodbye. Ain't nothing else to it. Better start at it backward. Think how it'll be rememberin' and thinkin' about her every day and not havin' her. Then she'll either go plumb off the handle and wind up in a padded cell or get well and marry somebody else. Either way, you lose." She humphed mightily and stamped off to the kitchen.

Frazer was still for a long time. Amanda had compressed the matter into two very near unassailable packages. He shrugged. The attractions of getting drunk had shrunk considerably. "Serve dinner," he yelled. "I've decided not to get drunk."

"I thought you'd smarten up sooner or later," she bellowed smugly.

CHAPTER SEVENTEEN

He went to work the next day feeling somewhat disembodied. Miss Murdock flitted in and out on errands as spurious as her curiosity was genuine until at last she erupted.

"All right, dammit, what happened yesterday?"

He looked up, his eyes troubled and serious. "Quite a lot, Gert. Mind if I don't talk about it today?"

"I mind, but I can see you mean it. All right. I'll go stew about it." She flounced out leaving him in a brown study.

He called Marvelle and was raddled with annoyance when she said she couldn't see him at the usual dating hour of eight o'clock.

"Well..." He frowned and twisted in his seat. "I mean, why not?"

"It's something I can't explain right now. If just wouldn't be convenient at that time."

"Who's there?" he barked, flushing with the realization that he sounded like a jealous schoolboy.

"Bern's here," she said cooly. "Mr. Frazer, I realize that I'm not the sort of person you'd care to trust much, but this time you'll just have to. I can't see you at eight and that's final." She hung up leaving him with an unvoiced apology that sat like a dirty sour rag on his stomach.

He sat at his desk and scowled at the blotter until his ears rang then abruptly he buzzed Miss Allen.

"I'm leaving for the day," he snapped. "If anyone wants me, I'll probably be at my place."

Miss Allen indicated that she understood and implied at the same time that he had been absent several hours the day before and why didn't he have to work just like anyone else? He left in a simmering rage, directed at his acerbic secretary, but springing from a number of other sources. He fumed and fretted about the apartment until Amanda shooed him out as soon as he had eaten dinner.

"And get drunk if you can't find nuthin else to do," she yelled at his departing back.

He began to walk and feeling somewhat relieved, decided to walk by the Huntingdon Tower and have a chat with the watchers if either Mazzarelli as there.

He found Sam leaning against a cab across the street from the Tower gossiping with the driver.

"What's good?" asked the big man grinning.

"Nothing," replied Frazer shortly. "You walking the beat today?"

"Yeah. I took over from Johnny. He's got two more men for the late shift. Nothing doing now. I guess he'll play it cool for a white."

"He should. He's drawn back a nub twice. What's with that lawyer and his friend?"

"The friend was unlucky. He was carrying a heater or he might have convinced a jury that he was just along for the ride. Miley and Matta will get time and Miley will be disbarred. Scimica went the easy way. That Wolff plays rough even if he is small." Mazzarelli straightened up and his quick inhalation was audible. "Well now. That's odd. I didn't know he ever attended to his own business."

"Who?"

"Hunt Harrington. He just went into the Tower lobby."

"Wolff's there, isn't he?"

"He was the last time I checked. Think we better amble up that way?"

"I think so," said Frazer and led the way.

They did not consider Hunt Harrington, singular, particularly dangerous so they didn't hurry. They had to wait for an elevator which delayed them further and by the time they got into the lift, Frazer was becoming nervous and his imagination was dealing him hard low blows.

Wolff smoked like a furnace and paced up and down, grimacing as he moved his cigarette from one side to the other.

"I wish you'd tell me what it's all about," asked Marvelle for the hundredth time.

"I can't tell you because I don't know," he told her patiently. "All I want you to do is stay away from us. Remember that."

"But why? What's going to happen?"

"How the hell do I know what's going to happen? Maybe nothing. Maybe he'll turn around and leave when he sees me. All I can do is hope."

The buzzer sounded and Wolff came alive with a snap. He made a furious gesture to banish her to the other side of the room and opened the door.

Wolff looked critically at the surprised Harrington, impeccable in a superbly tailored dark suit, dark blue tie and snowy white shirt. "Well, I didn't know you could dress slime up like that. Do come in."

Harrington flushed scarlet and came in slowly. Wolff closed the door with a quick movement and strode across the living room to confront Harrington again. Marvelle was pale and taut against the far wall.

"I understood you would be alone," he said suavely, ignoring Wolff.

"He wouldn't go," she said, her voice rather strident.

Harrington smiled easily. "Is that all? We can fix that easily enough." He turned to Wolff whose hands were jammed into his pockets so hard it appeared his jacket would come off. "We can dispense with your company. I have a proposition to make to Miss Martingale."

"I dare say," replied Wolff nodding as though in agreement. "However, the nature of such propositions as you have made other women of my knowledge has been of the sort that surgeons carry at arm's length and drop into an incinerator. You're slime, Harrington. You'll make no propositions to my client, either now or ever, so just turn yourself around and get out."

Harrington smiled and it was as stiff as bent tin. "Why is it that the smallest dog always barks the loudest? Wolff, your name I know because I took the trouble to find out. You're a nobody, a jackal hovering around the outskirts of a great art trying to absorb the rays rightly belonging to others." He made a smooth motion and slid a flat blue .38 automatic from beneath his arm. "Get out of here," he said metallically, "or you'll go out feet first."

Wolff, his eyes burning and sunken, stared at Harrington for a long moment. He walked the cigarette from one side of his mouth to the other. "Is that the way you want to play it, slime?"

"Don't tempt me, little man, or I might lose my temper."

Wolff's smile was a travesty. "For a gunman, you'd make a pretty good chiropractor. Your safety is still on. I therefore call your bluff. You've got a streak down your back the color of a ripe, ripe lemon. I spit on you." He did. It was a copious deluge that struck Harrington's forehead and trickled down to the point of his nose. The man's rage was a fearful thing to see. He went as white as whey and two lumps of muscle stood out on either side of his jaws. Wolff waited until he saw the thumb flick the safety downward, then he shot Hunt Harrington three times just to the left of the sternum. A fifty cent piece would have covered the holes. Harrington's face went blank, then contorted from a fearful wave of agony as it reached his reflexes. He took two stumbling steps forward, his gun going off as his finger stiffened on the trigger. He dropped the gun and very slowly collapsed on it.

Frazer and Mazzarelli heard the shots as they stepped out of the elevator and broke into a hard run. They hammered on the door until Wolff let them in.

"He's all there…mostly," said the agent. "He pulled a gun on me and I let him have it. You can ask Marvelle." He handed Mazzarelli the .32 automatic. "I'll go quietly after I've doused this fire in my coat pocket."

The big man looked at the girl. "I don't care how it happened," he said quietly. "Just for the record, how did it?"

"Just like Bern said." She smiled and Frazer was struck that she was free of any signs of panic or fear. In fact, he had the sneaking notion that she had rather enjoyed it. "Mr. Harrington pulled his gun… Now Bern might have helped things along the way he talked to him. He was furious when he pulled the gun."

Mazzarelli carefully turned the body on its side, looked at the three holes, smelled the muzzle of the .38 and let the body assume its original position.

"It'll cook fine, I think. I'll call homicide. They're not going to like having Wolff knock off two men and get away with it, but if they're still working with evidence, it'll work."

Wolff came out of the bathroom, his right coat pocket dark with water. "Just a small smudge," he said.

Frazer faced Marvelle. "You knew this was going to happen?" he said accusingly.

She smiled. "No. I knew something would happen. I knew he'd come up because I told him he could."

Mazzarelli chuckled. "Rigged, by God. I might have known it."

Wolff smiled grimly. "Looked like the only safe way out of the situation. I know that bastard. He'd have never given up." He looked hard at Mazzarelli. "Will it be necessary to tell your boys when they get here?"

Mazzarelli looked blank. "Sorry, son, I don't know what you're talking about. I heard Miss Martingale say something but I don't hear too good anymore."

Two hours later Wolff had answered questions from homicide for the second time in a few days. Tougher questions this time and more of them. How had he happened to be armed and waiting? Did he have a permit for the gun? How long had he known Hunt Harrington? Many more, but he answered them easily and with perfect calm.

They were gone now and only Mazzarelli, Frazer, Wolff and the girl were in the apartment. Mazzarelli got up and stretched hugely.

"Well, that was a neat lasting ending to what could have been a nasty thing." He cocked an eye at Wolff. "Don't go laying any more guntraps for solid citizens, Bern."

The agent's eyes were slaty. "I don't talk to ex-flatfoots who peddle their own scribble. I don't think any more traps will be necessary where this one is concerned." He tossed a glance toward Marvelle who was watching Frazer with a sort of breathless concentration. He was watching her in very much the same way but when Wolff spoke he straightened up and looked embarrassed. Wolff got up. "Let's get out of here, Sam. The air is stuffy."

Marvelle leaped to her feet and flew into Wolff's arms. "Bern, that was a wonderful thing you did tonight. I'll never forget it."

He patted her on a shoulder. "You'll forget it in a very short while. Youth has short memories because it has other things to think about. I'll call tomorrow."

Wolff and Mazzarelli went out and an uneasy silence settled between Frazer and the girl. She, however, was not disposed to allow it to last. She went over to him and placed a hand on his shoulder.

"Craine...I can call you that, can't I?"

He looked startled. "Of course. I've been wanting you to get off that Mr. Frazer business but when you come to think of it, we've never had a lot of association."

"We've had almost none. You've never had a date with me." She smiled mistily. "It doesn't feel that way … inside, I mean."

"No, it doesn't." He clenched his teeth in determination. "There's something I want you to listen to. Will you come over to my place?"

"Of course. Now?"

"Now."

Amanda was nowhere in sight when they arrived at Frazer's apartment, so he dug out his tape recorder, threaded the tape he was carrying into the mechanism and flipped the switch to play back and turned to her. His face drawn and taut.

"I went to see Leibermann about … well, the thing I had stuck in the back of my mind. He used something like truth serum and found that what I felt was not really a part of me but merely the product of conditioning. A conditioned reflex as it were. This is a tape of that session. I hate like hell to play it because it's a man without a defense to his name and some of it doesn't listen very good."

She put a hand on his arm. "Craine, you don't have to play that to me."

"I know I don't from your standpoint. Look at it from where I sit. Until you hear with your own ears exactly what I am basically, then you won't know that what happened to you might very easily happen to me, all things being equal. Do you understand?"

"Yes." Her eyes were starry wells of tear-drenched loveliness and Frazer swallowed jerkily. "Oh, Craine, this is such a wonderful thing you're doing. People just don't deliver to another person their defenses and step naked out before a cold world."?

"Maybe … I rather think you would. You haven't tried to excuse or justify a single thing you ever did." He smiled crookedly.

"I thought about that on the way to your place tonight. It cost me but I asked myself the question, 'I don't have to play this thing for her. I could throw it away but can I be any less than I know she'd be under the same circumstances?' "

She cuddled against him and sighed. "You even manage to turn it into a compliment for me."

"You've got a lot of them coming," he said profoundly. "You've got some apologies coming, too. You're about to listen to one."

"Please, please, *please* ... don't ever apologize to me for the way you felt. Be perfectly honest, how could you have felt any other way?"

"That's past," he said gruffly. "Listen to this."

She listened enthralled and several times her eyes brimmed and dripped tears.

When it was over, she kissed him as though it was to last through all eternity and sobbed a little through the electric contact. "I'll always remember listening to that, Craine ... and the reason why you let me."

"That's all done with now. Shall we keep it or burn it?"

"I think we should ... No. It's yours. You do what you wish with it."

"I think it should go in my vault at the ranch. Just knowing it's there will make me stay humble."

They sat on the couch and she took his arm, pulled it around her neck and placed a big hand over her right breast. The touch made her start a little, but she only sighed and cuddled closer.

"There's one thing we haven't talked about?" she said.

"What's that?"

"I'm still an alcoholic, you know."

"Want a drink?"

"No ... I really don't." She pressed his hand against her harder. "I have you and for some reason that seems to make a terrific difference, but I don't think we should assume that I'm cured."

"I'm going to take a sabbatical leave," he told her. "We've going to spend six months or a year travelling. You'll be with me all the time and together we're going to beat it."

She smiled up at him. "You know something? You haven't even told me you love me."

He told her and such was the proof he provided that fifteen minutes later, Amanda who had heard them but stayed in her room, came out on silent slippers and stopped short in the doorway. Her hand went to her mouth and if she had been able to blush she would have performed nobly. She backed up hastily and went back to her room closing the door softly.

"Wow," she said profoundly. "That's *some* gal. And I walked spang in on 'em just like any clumsy fool." She mopped her face and poured a drink of gin from a bottle she took from a chest of drawers. She raised the glass in the direction of the living room and gave a silent toast.

Two people sat at a kitchen table and looked blearily at each other.

"Bern," said Miss Murdock who was having trouble with her tongue. "A weddin' is a beau'ful thing, ain't it?"

"No," said Wolff sourly counting the glasses of champagne in his hand when he was morally certain he hadn't picked up but a single glass. "This damn stuff's mup ... mult'plyin' right in my hand."

"You're drunk," she accused.

"Sure. On his champagne. Great stuff. Cos' a for'une." Tears came to his eyes. "My li'l girl's gone with thad long st ... strang out Te'as bassard but ..." He straightened up. "She's comin' back. Tole me she was comin' back and know sumpn, Gert. Ruther have that girl's word on sumpn than a signed noterized sta'ment."

"Sure. Your contrack wi' 'er is signed with her word."

"Bes' damn contrack I got too," he finished morosely. "Pour some more bubbles in one of these damn glasses I'm holdin' Don't matter which."

The plane hummed southward high in the night air, singing a song of power. Marvelle held to her new husband as though she were afraid he'd fly out of the tiny window at his shoulder. She sighed happily.

"Private plane and all."

"Pop's. He sent it up for our use. It's a converted bomber."

She raised her eyes to his and said, "Craine, I don't have to pretend anything to you, do I ... I mean on account of what happened that night when I first met you?"

He clutched her hard. "You surely don't. I've been meaning to tell you that but we've been going around in such a mad circle ..."

"Thank you," she whispered. "Does the door to the cockpit lock?"

He laughed. "No. But Bert is the soul of discretion." He got up and going forward touched the lean leathery pilot on the shoulder. "Bert, you keep your eyes straight ahead and don't be making any unscheduled visits to the passenger's space."

Bert grinned, his teeth showing white in his mahogany face. "Man, flying this crate is a full time job. Don't worry about me."

He turned back to the cabin and Marvelle the marvel leaped into his arms with a glad little cry.

THE END